The Coming Home Cafe

Books by Gayle Pearson

FISH FRIDAY
THE COMING HOME CAFE

The Coming Home Cafe

GAYLE PEARSON

Atheneum   1988   New York

The author thanks Sheryl Fullerton for her editorial wisdom
and Beverly Burch for additional assistance and encouragement;
also Wally Pearson and Fran Pearson.

"Left My Gal in the Mountain" by Carson J. Robinson Copyright © 1929 by
Southern Music Publishing Co., Inc. Copyright renewal assigned to Peer
International Corporation; International copyright secured. All rights reserved.
Used by permission.

Atheneum
Macmillan Publishing Company
866 Third Avenue, New York, NY 10022
Collier Macmillan Canada, Inc.
Designed by Marjorie Zaum
First Edition
Printed in the United States of America
10 9 8 7 6 5 4 3 2 1
Library of Congress Cataloging-in-Publication Data
Pearson, Gayle.
The Coming Home Cafe/Gayle Pearson.
—1st ed. p. cm.
Summary: In the summer of 1933, fearing that the Depression will
never release its stranglehold on her family, fifteen-year-old
Elizabeth Turnquist leaves to ride the rails from town to town,
looking for work.
ISBN 0-689-31338-1
[1. Depressions—1929—Fiction. 2. Runaways—Fiction. 3. Swedish
Americans—Fiction.] I. Title.
PZ7.P32312Co 1988
[Fic]—dc19 88-3448 CIP AC

For my parents

The Coming Home Cafe

»» 1 ««

ELIZABETH SWALLOWED HARD AND SHOVED HER RIGHT HAND INTO her pocket as the two men in overalls carried the Vanhorns' old RCA Victrola phonograph down the front steps and set it under the Chinese elm tree. Next came the chartreuse divan, the hutch that once had contained their best china and silver, and the dining room table.

The front sidewalk, where she stood grasping her brother Waldo's bike by the handlebars, was spotted with fresh oil. "If Pa sees this . . ." she said. "You'd better get a bucket and wash it down."

"Yeah, yeah," he answered, working the wrench around a rusty bolt in the crank assembly.

She sighed heavily and shifted her weight from one foot to the other, slightly jarring the steadiness of her grip, which prompted Waldo to turn up to her a face daubed with grease and impatience.

"Liz, hold it *steady* so I can get a grip on."

"I'm sorry," she said, turning once again toward the Vanhorn house. "It's just . . . where do you suppose they are?"

She heard the strains of concern in her voice and wished she hadn't said anything as Waldo rose to his feet, wiped his hands on his navy overalls, and squinted into the sun. She didn't think a ten-year-old should have to spend his time worrying, but how could you protect a kid in times like these?

"I don't know," he said, shielding his vivid blue eyes with a hand smeared with grease. "Maybe they've moved someplace already. Will we ever see them again?"

"Oh, sure," Elizabeth replied, trying to sound certain. "We'll see them a lot, I bet." She knew how much he liked the Vanhorn boys, and didn't want to see him hurt by their absence.

"Lookit that," he said with a sneer. "Those guys are just dumping their good furniture and things on the grass like it was trash. I wonder who they work for."

"Now don't start in on the tough-guy act. They probably work for the city and they're just doing what they're told. They have to earn a living, too, you know."

"Huh," he grunted. "If nobody took that job, it wouldn't get done."

"That's true, isn't it?" She ran her fingers through the blond strands of hair hanging over his forehead. "How'd you get to be so smart? Now watch where you squirt that oil, and next time put down newspaper." Then she went back to thinking about the Vanhorns, how maybe the men had the wrong house, because Mr. Vanhorn still had his job as a Chicago city teacher, even if the city hadn't been able to pay him in months. They must have had something to fall back on.

In the front window of the Rosetti house across the street, the left half of one sister's wrinkled face and the right half of the other sister's face peered from behind lace curtains. Next door to them, out on the front steps, the Lizewskis crowded around a pitcher of lemonade. She hoped that they didn't think of the Vanhorn eviction as entertainment, even if entertainment was hard to come by these days.

She jumped at the sound of glass shattering and turned to look back at the Vanhorn house itself, where a path of broken bottles and jars littered the front sidewalk like jewels glistening in the sun. The men weren't even being *careful.*

At that moment a black pickup truck pulled up to the curb out in front, expelling half a dozen grim-faced Vanhorns onto the street. First they all stood there, staring at their stuff on the lawn. Then, one by one, they disappeared through the maze of beds and chairs and tables into the house. Mr. Vanhorn had always looked like a sad man to her, maybe because of the way his mustache drooped around the sides of his mouth. He looked even sadder just then, though, standing on the sidewalk with his arm draped around Mrs. Vanhorn's shoulder until he went inside. Then Elizabeth watched her own ma, her eyes red-rimmed, descend their front steps in a housedress and cut across the lawn over to Mrs. Vanhorn's side. Elizabeth looked down at Waldo fumbling with a screwdriver as her ma guided Mrs. Vanhorn back across the lawn and into their house.

Vera was the last one out of the truck, sliding off the seat of the cab to the street. Then she stepped over the curb and onto the front lawn, where she began to walk among the furniture, stopping to touch a piece here and there before she plodded up the front steps.

As though they'd received some mysterious signal or roll call, it seemed half the men in the neighborhood, including Elizabeth's father, Carl, converged on the Vanhorn house, pulling on socks and shoes as they hurried down front porches, like a small sloppy army. Elizabeth didn't follow Vera inside, as she normally would have done. There was too private a thing going on there. Instead, she patiently hung on to the handlebars while Waldo polished the chrome. After a while Vera came back out again, dragging a brown suitcase down the front steps with both hands. Elizabeth waited until Vera was near the back of the truck, then handed the bicycle over to Waldo.

"Here, let me help."

Vera accepted her offer without a word, her lips pressed together in a thin white line, her glasses slipping off the end of her nose as she and Elizabeth heaved the suitcase over the back of the truck.

"Why didn't you tell me?" It came out sounding like an accusation and that wasn't what she wanted at all. "I mean," she tried again, "you must have known for a long time, and, well . . ."

"It was a last-minute thing," Vera cut in crisply. "My dad tried everything." She fumbled for a loose strand of hair that had fallen across her forehead, twisting it back and tucking it into place with a bobby pin.

Elizabeth wiped her forehead, thinking about what to say next. She'd hoped for another explanation, like the house was being emptied for fumigation or even some type of quarantine. Anything except what Vera confirmed. The Vanhorns had moved into the neighborhood six months after her own family had, in 1919. Now, fourteen years later, in 1933, they were leaving and Elizabeth didn't know what to say.

"I . . . I guess you found another place, then." She ran her finger over a deep scratch in the black paint above the truck's fender.

Vera turned to look at her this time, sliding her glasses back up her nose. "We've found a three-room flat over on Wabash. It's not a bad-looking building on the outside, but it won't hold all our stuff. It's in the basement, you know, and the toilet doesn't flush right . . ." Her last few words were lost, as the Swensen brothers jolted the underside of a cabinet on the curb, scattering a heap of magazines onto the street.

"Come on," said Elizabeth, motioning with her head. "Let's get away for a minute."

Vera hesitated, picking at her fingernail. "All right," she said a moment later, shrugging, and followed Elizabeth to the side of her house.

Elizabeth leaned against the slats of wood in the building to keep her knees from shaking and tried to steady her voice. "I . . . I just wanted to know if you were going to say good-bye or anything."

Vera shrugged again, as if none of it mattered at all. "I suppose, sometime." She lowered her head and another wisp of hair slipped free down across her face, making her look twelve instead of fifteen. "Maybe I didn't want you to know."

Elizabeth nodded, relieved that Vera was starting to say something that mattered. She thought for a minute and then said, "Didn't you have anything to fall back on?"

Vera laughed drily, swiping at her hair with a grimy hand. "Fall back on," she repeated. "You mean hidden underneath a mattress or what? You don't know what it's like, that's all."

Elizabeth winced, trying to shake off what seemed like a rebuke. Maybe she didn't know what "it was like," but things hadn't seemed any worse for the Vanhorns than for anyone else. They were all having a hard time. She stabbed at the ground, still soft from the spring rain, with her bare toe.

"I wish you would've told me. Maybe we could've done something." She shoved her hands into her pants pockets, digging for the cool reassurance of a few pieces of loose change against her skin.

5

The look on Vera's face was not so reassuring. "I've got to go."

"But, Vera, when will I see you? I don't even know where you live!"

"I don't remember the exact address. It's over on Wabash, but way up. . . ."

Her voice was flat and composed and Elizabeth wanted to shake her. "Your dad should have gotten another job or left the schools if they weren't paying him, for gosh sakes!"

"He loved his work. And still does." A line of color inched its way up Vera's neck and into her face.

"I know. But my father loved *his* work and he sure wouldn't have stayed on at Pullman if they weren't going to pay him. He'd never work for nothing. It's foolish. Look what's happened to you!"

Vera stood up straight and tossed her head back. "We'll get by. We'll manage, and after he gets his back pay, we'll buy a bigger house."

"I'm sure you will. I . . . I didn't mean the way that sounded. It's just I don't want you to go. . . ." She reached out and touched her friend on the shoulder, as the air around them began to vibrate with the roar of the truck's engine.

"They're ready to go with the first load. I'd better help." Vera backed away without another word. Elizabeth watched help-lessly as her friend turned and marched across the lawn, then lifted herself into the back of the truck. She sat perched on the armrest of a sofa with her head down as the truck pulled away. Elizabeth didn't bother to wave because she knew Vera wouldn't look back.

She went inside, plodding up the hallway stairs to the land-ing, then climbed the wooden ladder to her room in the attic. She loved having the seclusion of the attic room, even if in midsummer the heat rose up from the rest of the house and hovered about her like a heavy vapor; on the coldest winter nights, the heat from the furnace in the basement never reached the attic at all, leaving it chilly and raw. Yet it was her own special place.

The one window in the room looked out over the street, which still hummed with activity around the Vanhorn house, or what had been their house. She hoped Vera would return in the pickup for another load and drop by to give her their new address. But she didn't really believe it.

She sat down on her bed, planting her feet flat on the hardwood floor, and stared up at the newspaper clippings she'd taped around the walls of her room: Amelia Earhart in the cockpit of the plane she'd flown across the Atlantic, Greta Garbo as a spy in *Mata Hari,* and a map of the World's Fair, the "Century of Progress," taking place down on Lake Michigan.

She thought again about Mr. Vanhorn and what Vera had said. Some people said he was a hero for staying on without pay, but look what sticking to his principles had done to his family. Maybe he knew he'd never get another job anyway, or perhaps he'd thought that any day now—just any day!—the money would come. And perhaps he had actually started to receive some of his back pay . . . only months too late for it to do much good. It was his idealism or stubbornness or ignorance that had taken her best friend away. Elizabeth shook her head sadly.

She got up and went to the window again, leaning out over the front porch the better to see the Vanhorn house. The street was almost empty now, except for a few kids playing ball and the iceman's truck disappearing around the corner.

Later that afternoon, Elizabeth's mother, Esther, teetered on the top rung of the stepladder, her head and shoulders concealed by the foliage of the willow tree. "I thought I'd cut some of the lower branches back. It's overtaking the whole yard and the lettuce won't get any sun. I wish the cherries were ripe. I'd bake a pie and take it over to cheer up the Vanhorns." The branch above her shivered and fell as she snipped it in half.

"I think I'll go over, anyway," added Esther, wiping her forehead on her sleeve. "There's sure to be something in the pantry I can take. You want to come along?"

"Maybe." Elizabeth picked up a stone and hurled it across the yard, already quite sure she wasn't ready to see Vera's new place with the broken toilet and God-knew-what-else. "It's a shame, isn't it?" she said. "They should have had something to fall back on." She grouped the branches that had fallen into a neat pile near the base of the ladder.

"It is a shame," said Esther. "Especially since Roosevelt just passed that home loan insurance thing, and the city's starting to pay its teachers." She tottered above Elizabeth, her voice muffled by the rustling of the branches.

Holding the ladder steady as her mother stretched for a branch high over her head, she thought about her talk with Vera. "We have something to fall back on, don't we?" She squinted up into the glare of the sun, waiting.

Esther snipped the branch with her shears, then mumbled, "Yes, we have a little something to tide us over." She rested her hands on her hips and sighed, gazing down at her daughter. "Now, don't you start worrying, Elizabeth. We'll be all right." As she turned and reached for another branch, the ladder suddenly careened forward, sending her crashing through foliage and tumbling to the ground. She looked up at Elizabeth and laughed, then gasped in surprise, reaching for her ankle.

Elizabeth ran into the house, opened the icebox, smacked a large chip of ice with a hammer, stuffed it into a towel, then hurried back to cover her mother's ankle. "Do you think it's broken?"

"For goodness' sakes, no! It's just my weak ankle. Goes back to my ice-skating days as a kid." She leaned back on her elbows in the grass, her rolled-up shirt-sleeves revealing sturdy tan forearms.

Elizabeth lifted the ice pack to examine her mother's foot. "I didn't know you had a bad ankle. It's turning colors already."

"In time for the Fourth of July." Esther smiled.

"Ma . . ." Elizabeth hesitated, sitting back on her heels. "I'm . . . I'm just glad we have something to fall back on, that's all. It's good to know, isn't it, that it can't happen to us?"

Esther leaned forward to stroke her daughter's hand. "These are hard times for everyone, Elizabeth. I know you know that, and you feel bad about Vera. We all do the best we can, and it doesn't help to worry." She tried to move her foot and winced in pain.

"I'll call Dr. Wharton."

"Thanks, but it's all right, really. I can call him later."

Elizabeth avoided her mother's face. After she helped her mother inside, she carried the stepladder down to the basement and set it against the wall. Then she hurried over to the shelves her father had built, where extra canned goods were stored during the summer and fall. The top two shelves were entirely empty; on the bottom shelf were two jars of stewed tomatoes and a jar each of peaches, apricots, and prunes.

She took the stairs to the upstairs pantry two at a time. Bags of rice, beans, flour, and sugar. A few cans of soup and apple sauce, a tin of lard, and a white wooden bin a third full of red and white potatoes. She stood looking at the empty places on the shelves. It's summer and there's the garden, she thought. She'd try to help out more, do all the watering and weeding until her mother's foot was better. Beyond that, she couldn't think of what more she could do.

She avoided the Vanhorn house for days, as if it were the "Big Bad Wolf" itself swallowing up families left and right, until finally she gave in to her curiosity one afternoon and went over for a look. Once inside the screened porch, she was able to peer through the curtainless windows. What had once been Vera's home was now only a vacant building.

Where exactly "on Wabash"? she wondered morosely. Vera had said "way up somewhere. . . ." The other end of Wabash, toward downtown, she knew was a slum full of tenements, winos, and flophouses. At least the Vanhorns hadn't disappeared in the middle of the night like the Rothmans.

She forced herself away from the window, out through the porch, and back down the front steps. As she crossed the front lawn her foot struck something hard in the grass and she bent to retrieve it. She recognized it right away as one of Vera's things, an old-fashioned brown medicine bottle. When she examined it more closely, a miniature, distorted reflection glinted back at her. She saw Vera's image in her mind, the blurry edges of her sad face dissolving into the glass.

2

ELIZABETH STEPPED OUT ONTO THE FRONT PORCH THE NEXT morning to take in the bottle of milk, but it wasn't in its usual place on the faded brown mat. She sighed, shielding her eyes from the sun edging over the tops of the houses across the street. The "Eight O'clock Gang" had struck once again. "They should be shot," she said to herself, letting the screen door bang loudly behind her.

" 'The Eight O'clock Gang' got our milk," she announced to her mother, Waldo, and two-year-old Whitney, all seated at the kitchen table. She was sorry to be the one to tell them, and she looked away when she did, because she knew how much it would pain her mother to pay Mr. Spinoso ten cents for something they never got. "They should be shot! Or worse!" she blurted, crossing the kitchen toward the stove.

"Elizabeth! They should be *caught,* not shot!" Esther lifted the coffee pot from the burner and went to the sink to fill it, leaning heavily on a homemade crutch.

"No, Ma. I'll do it; sit down." Elizabeth took the pot from her hand, filled it half full of water and set it back on the stove. When she reached for the handle of the icebox, she noticed a sheet of paper taped to the door. In her mother's handwriting, it said:

CONTEST

$1000 for naming the new Betty Crocker cake recipe! It's a chocolate cake, with peppermint flavoring and marshmallow icing.

Ideas for Names:
1. Choco-Mint Medallion
2.
3.
4.
5.

She stood in front of the refrigerator, thinking. It wasn't the first contest her mother had entered. She'd tried to win $500 by saying in twenty-five words or less why she'd changed to Oxydol; $100 for thinking of ten things to do with Jell-O; and there had been others.

"You don't even have to make the cake to win," Esther was saying as she hobbled her way to the table. "The ad said the average woman has a better chance of winning than a professional advertising man. Choco-Mint Medallion. What do you think?"

"I think it's a good start." She couldn't come up with anything clever herself and opened the icebox door. Hoping there would be even a tablespoon of milk in a bottle stuck back in a corner, she peered inside, but there wasn't. She didn't really mean that the thieves should be shot, of course. She just despised the thought of her mother drinking black coffee, and Waldo and Whitney eating dry oatmeal, because of some little hoodlum. The milk, along with somebody's loaf of bread now and then, just seemed to vanish from people's porches. No one leaving for work ever happened on a thief sneaking out of the bushes, and no dogs ever barked a warning. She thought she would have liked to catch one of the thieves herself, find out what kind of person would steal from poor people. She drew in her breath, wondering how she could have thought such a thing! They weren't *poor*, really—just having a hard time because of the way things were.

As she lowered the flame under the pot, she remembered the plot of a movie she'd recently seen, a trap set for somebody's gangster-boyfriend, and wished she could think of a clever way to catch the milk thieves herself.

"Coffee's coming right up," she said to her ma, setting a cup down before her on a bare table top spattered with gray clumps of oatmeal. She threw Waldo her most disgusted look and grabbed a spoon from Whitney's small hand. "Waldo! You should know better than to waste food like that! Ughh!"

He scowled and tilted his chair back against the wall; Whitney struggled free of her grasp and scrambled away from the table. She could hardly blame either of them, though, for dueling with their spoons instead of eating the rubbery paste in their bowls. It looked like something she'd once used in art class to make paper-mache animals.

"Let's get breakfast over and those newspapers out. I have other things to do, you know." She slumped beside Waldo with a slice of bread and black coffee.

"Like what?" he asked, drawing an imaginary picture on the table with the end of his spoon. "Going to the movies?"

"How nice," said Esther. "Elizabeth's going to help you again. What a good sister."

"Yes, the movies! And I don't even care what's playing. It'll be cool inside, that's all."

"I don't like you just having coffee plain like that without no milk," said her ma. "It'll stop you from growing."

"Huh," she said, stretching her legs out under the table. "I think I'm done growing, but I don't like it this way, either. Too bitter." She made a sour face, lowered her head halfway to the table and brought the cup to her mouth. Sipping the steaming liquid loudly, she thought that her mother probably didn't know that helping with the papers helped her out in a way, too, because it made her feel as if she were at least doing something. Besides delivering papers, Waldo got to polish brass doorknobs over at the "Y," but that was in exchange for a free membership, which pleased their father very much. Carl had said as soon as things got better he was going to buy Waldo a pair of boxing gloves so Waldo could train and really "learn how to handle himself."

"Your foot's not much better, is it?" Elizabeth didn't look at her ma, studying the wall straight ahead of her instead, which was decorated with a china plate from Sweden sent over by her father's aunt for the holidays one year. "Did you call the doctor?"

Out of the corner of her eye she saw her mother picking at a loose thread on the sleeve of her terrycloth robe. "Oh, it's a little better," said Esther. "I'll give it another day or two. He's busy and I don't want him to think I'm a hypochondriac or something. Don't you wonder, if you pulled and pulled on this strand, if you'd end up with just a pile of thread and nothing more?" She laughed, and so did Waldo.

"You'd look like a dummy in a store window without no clothes on," he teased.

"I hope I'd look nicer than *that.*"

Elizabeth took her coffee into the living room, where her father had spread newspapers on either side of him on the sofa.

"Nothing," he complained. "Not a damn new thing."

"*Carl,*" Esther warned from the kitchen.

"I might as well never look. And if there's something promising, you know a thousand guys will beat me to it. And better qualified, too!"

"Oh, Pa. You'll get something," said Elizabeth. She stood awkwardly in the middle of the room, thinking she had wanted to sit beside him for a while, but now, seeing the scowl on his face, the way his uncombed hair wilted across his forehead, she knew she didn't.

"*Ja, ja,* sure. . . ."

She was glad she had the newspaper delivery to get her out of the house. Her father would go through the job ads three or four times at least, then pace the floor, curse Roosevelt's New Deal because it hadn't gotten him a job yet, and end up brooding in a corner, talking Swedish to himself. The air hung heavy around him these days, like the thick, black factory smoke curling up from the steel mills south of the city. When he'd first lost his Pullman job he figured he'd get another tool-and-die-maker job right away. For a while he resorted to selling insurance door-to-door, then encyclopedias. When he couldn't sell enough of either, he tried sports equipment at T. J.'s Department Store and when T. J.'s went under, he worked evenings as a part-time janitor at the State Theater. He'd planned to pick up something else in the daytime, like a job at the new brewery that opened in March over on Throop, but they were taking younger men and the "something else" never came along. Elizabeth was happy that her father got an employee's movie pass, but she was sorry for what he had to do to earn it.

The sweat streamed down her back as she and Waldo took turns dragging the wagon over the cinders along the tracks. They'd peddled most of the extra papers in front of Walgreen's and she'd managed to keep him out of fights with other newsboys

15

over who got to stand in the choicest spots. Now she was exhausted, just wanting to get home, wash up, have a glass of lemonade, and head for the matinee.

Their eyes glued to the tracks for chunks of coal that might have slipped off a passing train, they didn't even see the kid picking his way between the ties with a pack slung over his shoulder until they were almost face-to-face.

"Bums," said Waldo, once they'd passed him and he was out of earshot. "I seen a lot of 'em lately."

"I think they're called 'tramps' at that age." She said it in a soft voice, just to make sure the kid couldn't hear. " 'Bums' is for when they've been doing it a while."

"That's right," her brother said, as Elizabeth turned to glance at the boy's back. "Bums have whiskers and drink a lotta whiskey." He began to weave to his right and his left, staggering in a drunken imitation.

Elizabeth laughed and poked him in the arm as they turned off the tracks at 111th. When they reached the end of their block, she saw the ice truck parked alongside the curb about halfway down the street. Waldo started walking straight again, and fast, the wagon bumping along the sidewalk behind him.

"Now, Waldo . . ." she started, hurrying to keep up. "Someday that truck is going to pull away with you in the back and we'll never see you again! Maybe *nobody* ever will, because that guy's from Russia!"

She thought what she said must've gone into his bad ear, the one pierced by a BB shot the summer before. He dropped the wagon handle and crept around to the front of the truck to make sure Ivan wasn't inside the cab, then hurried around the other side and hopped up onto the back.

"I'm only doing my part." He cupped his hand over his mouth and whispered down, "We need the ice. C'mon, we do.

And he can't sell the small stuff, anyway, so it's not even stealing."

He disappeared behind a large block, only to reappear a moment later. "There *are* no small chips," he said with impatience.

"Let's go!" Elizabeth hissed, looking over both shoulders. She put her hands on her hips, trying to show him she meant business.

"Just hold your horses," he gasped, kneeling behind the block of ice. "It'd go faster if you'd give me a hand. . . ." She took a step back in retreat as he started pushing. The ice tumbled to the pavement and shattered into hundreds of pieces, and in seconds kids came running up to the truck from all around the neighborhood. "Yea, Waldo, yea, Waldo!" they sang. They knew it was Waldo without looking.

"Yea, *Woldo.*"

It was Ivan the iceman, appearing out of nowhere from the side of his truck. "Yea, Woldo, yea, Woldo," he mimicked again, picking Waldo up and dangling him by the collar like a thin sausage. "This time your mother, next time the cops!" His huge, red nose was inches from Waldo's face. Then he let Waldo drop to the street with a thud and charged with his fists flailing at his side to the Turnquist house, where Elizabeth knew he'd collect twenty-five cents from Esther for a block of ice she wasn't going to get.

Elizabeth went around to the back of the house for a drink from the garden hose, knowing that bad things came in threes and the day wasn't over. She had changed her mind about the lemonade, not wanting to see the disappointment on her mother's face or to see Waldo get a whipping from Pa. Instead she headed straight for the State Theater. As she passed the small shops on Michigan Avenue, she kept worrying about Waldo; all the way to his ruin, he would say he was "only doing his part."

⇢≫ ≪⇠

What she loved most about the movie theater was its cave-like atmosphere, its cool darkness, how it gathered her up and transported her to another world. And she didn't have to do anything to get there, just sit and watch, and be carried away to wonderful, romantic places where there were no breadlines. She didn't even need the dime to get in, because her father got the free pass, and he always let her use it.

She settled into a cushioned seat near the front of the theater, as *Queen Christina*, with Greta Garbo, was just beginning. For an hour and a half she hardly moved at all, until the end, when Garbo turned to bid her sweetheart good-bye, saying, "In the future, in my memory, I shall live a great deal in this room." Elizabeth dried her eyes with the back of her hand, hoping no one around her was watching.

She'd seen the next film, *Mata Hari*, before, so all the way through it she knew that Garbo would stand before a firing squad in the end, dying to protect her lover. Long after the screen had gone dark, she remained in her seat, staring ahead, having felt the bullet pierce her own chest and the life drain out of her. She did not know how a person gave up her own life for someone else. Was it courage or lack of fear? Or the kind of love adults meant, when they talked about being "in love"?

When finally she dragged herself up out of her chair, down the aisle, and into the lobby, the first person Elizabeth saw was her father coming toward her in his overalls, with a long-handled broom and a trash barrel. She was sure he didn't see her slip into the rest room.

⇢⟫ 3 ⟪⇠

MRS. VANHORN AND ESTHER WERE SIPPING ICED TEA ON THE FRONT porch when Elizabeth arrived home from the library. The streets were empty and she suspected that everyone else had escaped to the beaches to catch a lakefront breeze, as the summer of '33 was turning out to be one of the hottest on record. She liked the library because it was cool and dark, like a movie theater, and she could lose herself in a good book just as easily as she could in a good movie.

As she approached the front steps she felt she ought to offer some sympathy to Vera's mother, as though someone had died. She didn't think it seemed right to say she was *sorry* they'd lost their home, but she had to say something. She couldn't look the other way, as she had done the day the Vanhorns moved, almost six weeks ago.

Esther smiled up at her daughter. "We have company, Elizabeth. Guess who's here."

Elizabeth thought it was a silly thing to say when she was standing right in front of Mrs. Vanhorn, until she *really* looked at her. Then it didn't seem so stupid, because she might not have recognized Mrs. Vanhorn passing her on the street. Her clothes were neat and her hair combed and clean, but her face was thin, hollow in places, and pallid. Her dress hung loosely about her shoulders as though it were still on the hanger. Elizabeth looked to her mother, shocked and speechless.

"The Vanhorns' flat is over on Wabash near the Monarch Cleaners, so Vera can still go to Southridge."

Elizabeth nodded, seeing in her mother's eyes an appeal that she say something kind and say it quickly. "I know where that is . . ." she began.

"We've missed having you around so much. You and all your family."

Just hearing Mrs. Vanhorn's voice made Elizabeth realize how much she'd missed them, too. "I hope you're all okay in your new . . . place," she said.

"We're getting by. We just thought we'd drop by for a chat. You're looking more like your dad every day."

"We?" asked Elizabeth.

"Vera's waiting out in back. I'll bet you can find her under your willow, on a day like this. Whew. . . ."

"Oh good," said Elizabeth, trying for the right combination of enthusiasm and indifference. She turned and took the stairs calmly, then hurried through the living room and dropped her books on the table. Through the kitchen window over the sink she saw the once-familiar sight of Vera cross-legged on the old chenille bedspread under the weeping willow. For a moment she stood there at the window; then she turned to open the icebox, removed the pitcher of lemonade, and poured two tall glasses. She kicked the back door open with her foot and went down the back step into the yard.

Vera looked up from her magazine as Elizabeth crossed the lawn. "Mother wanted me to come along. I would have preferred the beach myself," she called out.

"So would I," said Elizabeth. She handed her friend a glass and lowered herself onto the bedspread. "But I didn't want to go alone."

"What about Marcia? Can't you do anything with her?"

"She's baby-sitting. Every day, all day. What magazine is that?"

"*Movie Mirror,*" Vera replied. "There's a special photo story on Marlene Dietrich."

"Your mother let you pluck your eyebrows. I thought she was against that sort of thing!"

"Yeah, I don't know why she changed her mind and let me. Maybe it was a consolation prize." She shifted her head from side to side. "What do you think?"

"I like it. It makes you look older." Elizabeth wanted to ask Vera about her ma looking older, and not very well, but she couldn't think of how. She tore a handful of grass from the ground and looked off into the next yard. "So—how have you been?"

"Oh, you know. Okay, I guess, considering. Look at this advertisement!" She flipped the magazine around so Elizabeth could see a photo of Mary somebody, a famous stunt girl, doing a midair suspension glide from an airplane, hanging only by her teeth.

" 'Camels never give me edgy nerves, even when I smoke a lot,' " Elizabeth read. "Gee, do you think you'll ever smoke?"

"Maybe," Vera replied, flipping another page. "Isn't she something, though?" She pointed to a photograph of Marlene Dietrich in a white tuxedo and top hat. "Isn't that fine? I'm going to save up for something like that myself." She swatted a fat, noisy fly near her face and her glasses slid to the end of her nose.

"It looks great on her. I'm not so sure how I'd look in it. Like

21

a clown, I imagine." Elizabeth laughed, but it felt forced and unnatural, not like the old times. She searched Vera's face for a clue as to how she really was. "Why don't you use my pass to get into a movie? They don't check names. I've seen a lot of movies that way myself."

Vera moistened her thumb and turned a page, as though she hadn't heard.

Elizabeth bit her lip, realizing she'd said the wrong thing. "You should see Garbo in *Mata Hari,*" she said. "Vera, she's really something, you know. Who could be tougher? To face a *firing squad* and . . . oops! I gave away the ending." She covered her mouth.

"That's okay. I probably won't go." Vera flipped another page and then another. "Dietrich. She's tougher than Garbo, I think. Hardly ever smiles, and when she does, it's at somebody else's expense."

"You know, Vera, maybe your ma could use the pass."

"Maybe. You could ask her yourself."

"I will, then. Is she feeling okay? Your ma?"

Vera lifted her chin, as though she were defending herself, and looked into Elizabeth's face. "She's fine. It's the heat. Makes her tired out."

"Uh-huh. It is tiring. She just looks thin and all. . . ."

"It's the hottest summer, you know. But she's tough. Tougher than Garbo and Dietrich together." Vera briskly tossed the magazine aside and focused on the fingernails of her left hand.

"Yes, she is tough," Elizabeth agreed. Maybe she was, but she sure didn't look it. It was the kind of thing she might have said aloud to Vera before, but now there was something between them, something more than what had been put there by time and distance. And she was afraid, suddenly, that it was catching, like typhoid. Maybe it was being poor. She didn't know. Inhaling

22

deeply, she tried to take herself out of the summer of '33 altogether, to remember what it had been like before, but she couldn't. The smell of the fertilizer in her mother's garden kept her right where she was.

Her mother loved flowers, and they'd always had a yard full of peonies and pansies, sweet Williams and marigolds, irises, tulips, and roses. Now there were carrot tops poking through the crusty earth, tomato plants crawling up homemade trellises, rows of lettuce and corn where the pansies had been. She gave half of the fresh vegetables away, not because they didn't need the food themselves, but because she thought others needed it more. On more than one occasion Elizabeth had helped her mother bag the stuff and carry it down to the 103rd Street soup kitchen.

"Maybe you should take your ma to the doctor," Elizabeth suggested.

Vera's eyes grew big under her newly plucked eyebrows. She shook her head in silence.

"Just in case . . ." The rest of the sentence slipped away. Elizabeth was trying to bridge the gap between them by speaking from her heart, but she could tell by Vera's tight-lipped silence that it wasn't working. "I thought the city was paying its teachers again," she wanted to say, but didn't.

"It's probably nothing," she said instead. "She is tough, your ma. She'll be okay. How're your new house and neighborhood? Made any new friends?"

"Steven sleeps in the bathtub because he's afraid of mice. He thinks they're rats, and maybe they are. I don't know, except that I can hear something scratching around at night." She said it half crying, yanking the grass from the ground in huge tufts.

"Oh!" said Elizabeth. "That's horrible!" She picked up the magazine, sorry she'd asked, and leafed through it quickly. But she couldn't stop what came creeping into her mind then, no

23

matter how many photos of Dietrich she saw, or how fast she turned the pages. She could see little Steven curled up in the bathtub of a small, dark apartment, and a rat's tiny, slitted eyes and razor-sharp teeth, as it scurried around the floor and tried to climb up the sides of the porcelain tub. It nibbled at the edges of her consciousness until it was staring her right in the face.

"Are you going to the Fair?" Elizabeth blurted, yanking again at the grass around the bedspread. "I've saved over ninety cents collecting milk bottles, but I think I'll wait till I have more." She tried to picture Waldo and herself flying through the air on the Rocket Ride, but Vera was staring at her now with wide, strange eyes, like an injured animal.

"Did you know," she blurted again, unable to help herself, "that they have television at the Fair? It's like a small movie screen. They say someday everyone will have one. Can you imagine seeing Joan Crawford and Clark Gable kiss in your own living room?"

Vera slowly drew herself up, swaying back and forth until she gained her balance. She stood, blocking the sun, casting a shadow across the bedspread. Elizabeth stared at her kneecaps, waiting for Vera to go, and wanting her to, because she didn't want to know anymore about Vera's new life.

"Going to . . . to the *Fair?*" Vera stammered. "You . . . you know, you ought to look at your *own* mother. She doesn't look so well, either!" A few seconds later, she turned away without another word, her footsteps rustling in the tall grass alongside the house.

Elizabeth stared morosely at the ruts in the ground, where she'd pulled up the grass. How could she have been so rude? Vera had finally been ready to talk, and she'd shut her out. What kind of a friend would do that?

Elizabeth put her head in her hands and tried to think. Why

had this happened to the Vanhorns in the first place? They hadn't done anything wrong, and Vera's dad was kind of a hero. Maybe there *was* something else, some bad thing one of the Vanhorns had done, and God was getting even? But she didn't really think so.

→»» 4 «««←

"AAH, YOU DON'T KNOW WHAT GOOD IS!" CARL TURNQUIST laughed and dropped a thin piece of fish down his throat, swallowing it like a trained seal. He'd found a whole "fin," a five-dollar bill, sweeping up at the theater, and he'd splurged on two 39-cent jars of pickled herring and a bottle of beer. "Yeah, c'mon try it, it's good!"

Esther smiled weakly from across the table and sighed, as though she were indulging a child. "It's all yours, Carl," she said with resignation.

Elizabeth looked down at the mound of potatoes flecked with carrots and corn in the center of her plate. She'd already figured that 39 cents could've bought four bottles of milk, or seven loaves of bread, or two dozen eggs. She looked at her mother's plate. There was hardly anything on it. She wrinkled her nose, not fond of the smell of herring.

"Things will get better, you watch. This Roosevelt is a good man. He's not going to let people starve. I heard things are picking up already. Only way to get us out of this is to give us jobs. That fin I found is an omen. You watch." He tilted his head back and swallowed another fish.

Elizabeth glanced across the table at Waldo slumped over his food, toying at it listlessly with his fork. "Eat," she said softly across the table. "And quit slouching or Pa will yell." Scowling, the boy drew himself up and leaned into the back of his chair. "Your sister's right," said Esther. "Eat all the food on your plate so you're not hungry later."

She used to tell them to eat everything or they wouldn't get a snack before bed. How could her pa be celebrating anything?

Carl slapped his knee and took a swig of beer, starting in about getting his old job back at Pullman. "*Ja*, now that booze is legal, there'll be more money for everyone. Then your mother is going to have a new dress, a new hat, anything she wants." He pulled four one-dollar bills from his shirt pocket and waved them in the air like miniature flags. "And now get ready; we're going to the Fair!"

"Pa!" said Elizabeth. She laid her fork down. "Why don't we put the money away? Save it for . . . for . . ."

"Yippee," sang Carl. "Waldo and me on the Rocket Ride!"

"I don't want to go," Waldo said.

"Save the money, Pa," Elizabeth tried again. She looked to her mother for help. Why didn't she say anything?

Her father looked at her, grinning. "Then you come, Elizabeth. You're too serious these days. You need to have fun! We'll go to Treasure Island and eat hot dogs!"

"Carl," said Esther. "Elizabeth's right. Just put it away for a rainy day. You never can tell." She dabbed at her mouth with her napkin.

"Never can tell *what?*" said Carl. His smile had fizzled. "Can tell *what?*" He looked at Elizabeth. "Your ma always says that, you know. 'You never can tell, you never can tell.' " He pointed to Esther as if she were a statue, a *thing*, and not a person who had ears and could hear. "Can tell what, Esther? Whether the sun will shine? Whether the birds will sing? Or poop on your head instead?" He rolled up the four one-dollar bills and stuffed them back into his shirt pocket, folding his arms across his barrel chest. "You think a few dollars will save us? It won't."

"Carl," Esther said firmly.

"*Ja, ja.*"

Elizabeth gripped the sides of her chair. As the summer had slipped by, July into August, she had the terrible sense that they were slipping away, too, that they ought to do something and do it fast. But she didn't know what.

Esther raised her head, glancing uncertainly at the list on the icebox door. "Let's work on the contest. Think of it—a thousand dollars, just for a name. Choco-My-Heart. How about that?"

"Big Chocolate Deal," said Carl.

"Oh, c'mon, Carl," said Esther, dabbing at her mouth again. "Think of what a thousand dollars could do. You'd get your name in the paper, too."

"Big Chocolate Deal," he repeated, amusement spreading across his face. "After the New Deal."

"C'mon, Elizabeth," Esther urged. "Help us."

Elizabeth raised a spoonful of potatoes to her mouth. "Peppermarsh . . ." she suggested listlessly.

"She's not interested," said Carl. "She's not even trying."

"I am too trying, Pa. I'm just thinking out loud, trying to get the ingredients in."

"Choco-Mess," said Waldo. "I'm thinking, too."

"Well, don't." Elizabeth kicked him under the table.

"Ouch! Choke-Me-Chocolate and Peppermint Pig-O." He stuck out his tongue.

Carl threw his head back and laughed, drowning another fish in a swirl of beer. Whitney clambered to his feet on the chair, as his diaper dropped to his ankles. "Piggy, Piggy!" he shouted, swinging his hand into his milk glass.

"Oh, my," said Esther, rising from her chair.

"I'll get it." Elizabeth was halfway to the kitchen before Esther could finish protesting.

"Fat Chance Chocolate!" Carl hollered after her. "That's what I say. *Fat Chance Chocolate!*"

Elizabeth wrung out a dishcloth and brought it back to the dining room. "Somebody has to win." She swiped at the milk running toward the groove in the table, suddenly feeling better, even hopeful. "Ma's right. It could be us, Pa, if we keep on thinking."

"What about that shampoo contest?" he persisted. "Your mother tried it and it turned her hair green. Ha! Remember, Waldo? Stop kicking the table!"

Esther blushed. "We don't have to test anything. Just use our noggins. You never can tell."

"Oh, is that right?" Carl glared at her, his face flushed a bright red, oil from the fish lingering in a thin stream on his chin. "You look like a clown, Esther. Too much rouge."

Elizabeth turned to her mother and saw he was right. She looked like a porcelain doll, two bright crabapple patches of pink against ivory cheeks, like Mrs. Vanhorn. Was her mother sick, too? Suddenly Elizabeth felt sick herself and wished she could leave the table. She hated arguments during dinner and felt one coming on.

Her mother rubbed her hand across her cheek, trying to even out the color.

"Just a minute," said Carl. He was staring at Esther's left hand, which she let drop into her lap, like a weight had pulled it down.

"Your ring," he said. "Where is it?"

She met his gaze directly. "Not now, Carl. Dinner is not the time."

"Where is *your ring?*" His voice shook. His hand beside his plate began to tremble. As she rose from the table, so did his fist, descending in a crunching blow. Plates, spoons, and forks leaped into the air, flying everywhere.

"I told you I would get the money! What will you sell next, our children?"

Waldo leaned forward, thrusting his head down, gagging like a sick cat. A chunk of half-chewed food tumbled forth onto his plate; then he shoved his chair backward and charged out the kitchen door.

Elizabeth watched the screen door slam and then turned toward Whitney, who had begun to cry. She heard her ma running across the room and up the stairs, then she listened for footsteps overhead. The floorboards shuddered and Elizabeth guessed her ma had thrown herself onto the bed. She turned and picked up Whitney, who was crying harder than ever, pulled his diapers back on, and tried to soothe him. The child began sucking his thumb, staring hard into her face.

"Pa . . ." she began, her voice quivering. Her mouth and throat felt dry as dust.

"Her *wedding* ring. *Wedding* ring. How could she do it?" He held up his own left hand and looked at it hard, as if the thin gold band would tell him something he needed to know. He shook his head when he didn't get an answer and left the table, tramping heavily across the living room and out the front door.

Elizabeth awoke sometime during the night. The sounds of her father's cursing and crashing about the living room were making their way to the attic, through the heating vent. She couldn't remember his coming home drunk since he'd lost his job at Pullman. After a while it was quiet again and she figured he'd passed out on the sofa, but she couldn't go back to sleep until she'd made up her mind about something.

$\rightarrow\!\!\!\ggg$ 5 $\lll\!\!\!\leftarrow$

ELIZABETH STOOD BEFORE THE FULL-LENGTH MIRROR IN THE UP-
stairs hallway near her parents' bedroom, taking one deep breath
after another. It was Monday morning. She'd plaited her hair into
a single braid and pinned it to the back of her head. "Girl—
Swedish, neat: cook, housework, references. Stay. $3–4 week,"
the ad in the Sunday paper had said. She wasn't sure what the
"stay" meant. Stay for dinner, stay overnight, stay for the rest of
her life?

She drew her lips into a tight, round circle and clasped her
hands in front of her. She thought she still looked too young and
more like her ninth-grade music teacher than how she supposed
a nanny should look.

"I'm here to apply for the 'Swedish girl' job," she whispered.
"*Yob*. De Svedish girl *yob*. Not only have I been one my whole
life, but I'm also neat and do housework and I would like four
dollars a week instead of three. *Ja*."

She took a deep breath to calm herself and tiptoed down the stairs. Once she'd realized what she had to do, she'd felt a surge of determination and vigor. Of course it was the right thing. Why hadn't she thought of it sooner? She'd already wasted most of the summer.

Four dollars a week would buy lots of groceries, help to pay the mortgage. It would pull them up from the place they were dropping down to, like a rope thrown to a drowning person.

She left her parents a note on the kitchen table, saying she was seeing friends from school and would be home in time for dinner, knowing she'd have to think of someone to visit to keep the note from being an outright lie. She knew what they'd say if she told them she was looking for work. They'd starve before they let her quit school. Well, almost.

Her mother's purse lay on the counter. Elizabeth thought glasses would make her look older, and that her mother might not miss hers in the daytime. Slipping the glasses out of the purse, she noticed an envelope, saw it was addressed to Mrs. Eleanor Roosevelt, and not yet stamped or sealed. She pulled the envelope out and opened it, wondering why on earth her ma would be writing to the president's wife, and what she would say if Esther should enter the kitchen just then. She went on anyway, unfolding the paper and reading:

Dear Mrs. Roosevelt,

I am sorry to be bothering you. I know you are a very busy woman, what with your husband being president, and your newspaper column. And I wouldn't be writing at all if it was not serious, and if it was only me I was worried about. My husband lost his job a few years back like so many other people. He's only working a few hours a week. It's not enough to get by on. We're falling behind on the mortgage and I'm afraid we'll end up put out on the street with nowhere to go if we don't get help. I was wondering if we could get some special help with our home loan, as I'm sure he'll have a good job soon, and we'll repay anything we get. Anything you can do I would greatly appreciate.

Also, I hate asking, but do you know of any place I can get some winter coats for my three children? They've outgrown their old ones and winter will soon be here.

Respectfully,
Mrs. Esther Turnquist

She stared at the note in disbelief, returned it to the envelope, and then put it back in its place in her mother's purse.

The streetcar rattled and clanged its way up Cottage Grove Avenue. She guessed that the people whose heads were buried in newspapers had had the same jobs for years. It surprised her to see that for many folks maybe nothing had changed. Being among them made her feel good, secure, and important, and she wondered what it would be like to take her own paycheck home at the end of a week.

At 55th Street she rang the bell for a stop, stepped down to the curb, and started walking, thinking all the way about the look on her mother's face when she handed over that first check. Maybe she would cash it first and stop at the market. She knew just what she would buy, too. Meat. She could see a huge pot roast smothered in onions on a platter in the center of the table, and she saw her family's faces as they each heaped a portion onto their plates. Even Whitney would stop jumping around and eat.

Elizabeth found that she'd walked the few blocks to the address listed in no time at all and was almost unaware of her surroundings. When she really looked up and down the block, she was amazed at the size of the houses. How long would it take to mow a lawn that looked as large as the baseball diamond at Comiskey Park?

She rang the bell on Hyde Park Avenue. Her heart began to pound so wildly in her chest she thought she would probably faint or at least not be able to talk. To tell someone face-to-face that she thought they ought to hire her when there were so few jobs seemed like such a bold thing to do! But she didn't care what they thought. She would do it anyway, because she *had* to. At the last moment, she remembered her mother's glasses and slipped them out of the pocketbook and onto her nose.

The door opened. "Have you come to apply for the job?"

She squinted. It was like trying to see through a window streaming with rain. As she tried to make out the woman's face, she managed to stammer "*Ja*, I have."

She blinked and blinked, trying to see more clearly, as the maid ushered her into a parlor crammed full of other applicants. She peered at them over the rims of her mother's glasses. Most were older, maybe sixteen to twenty. They were all blond, though, and probably Scandinavian.

After the maid disappeared down the hallway, the stillness in the parlor was broken only by the whirring of three small fans set on tables around the room. Elizabeth would have liked to find out something about the other girls, but it was too hot to talk, and she wasn't sure she wanted to know anything about her competitors anyway. She might have liked to see what the room looked like, too, but she couldn't see anything. Her eyes ached.

One by one the girls were called for by the maid and led down a long hallway. Each time the maid returned, Elizabeth was afraid her name would be called and afraid it wouldn't. By the time her turn had come, a thin, dark line of sweat ran down the back of her dress to the end of her spine.

3 5

"Miss Turnquist, please."

The maid stood stiffly at the end of the hall. Elizabeth had arrived promptly at eight, and now it was half past ten. The interview room was a small office at the far end of the hall. A woman in a gray tailored suit was seated behind a desk. She smiled. Elizabeth squinted to see her and adjusted her glasses as she sank into a cushioned chair.

"I'm Mrs. Bright," said the woman. "I'm pleased to meet you, Miss Turnquist. My husband is a patent attorney who also teaches at the university. We have three small children, and we need someone to care for them, as you know."

Elizabeth was so nervous she felt like laughing. Three Bright children.

"Have you ever worked before?" asked Mrs. Bright.

Elizabeth shook her head, biting her lower lip.

Mrs. Bright made a little note with a pencil and continued. "Swedish on both sides?"

"Just one." Her mouth was dry as dust again, her tongue clinging to the roof of her mouth. "My mother's part Irish."

Mrs. Bright nodded slowly. Elizabeth strained to read her expression.

"Are you used to attending to small children? How old are you?" She had her pencil poised, ready to write.

"Fif . . . sixteen, and I have two younger brothers. I take care of them all the time. My mother depends on me. . . ." She leaned forward, squeezing the fingers of her left hand until they turned blue.

"I see; that's good. Now, are you an energetic sort of person or do you require an afternoon nap? What are you going to do about school, and do you have plans for some sort of career?"

Elizabeth answered all the questions slowly, giving herself time to think. She had plenty of energy, never took naps. Of course she would have a career. Someday. Later on, when things had changed. School? Well, she would get back to that, too. She thought that she was doing well until Mrs. Bright asked her about the five food groups needed to provide a nutritious meal. She squeezed her fingers again, trying to pull from her memory Mrs. Bean's seventh-grade lecture on nutrition.

"Meats, vegetables, fruits . . . grains . . ."

What had she forgotten? She later recalled it was dairy products.

"Hmmm," murmured Mrs. Bright. She seemed to be frowning. "Do you have your own cookbook or do you carry your recipes around in your head?" She looked at Elizabeth and waited, pencil tapping her note pad.

Elizabeth removed her glasses and wiped them with a handkerchief from her purse. She had not one recipe in her head, except perhaps for her mother's mayonnaise cake, which she didn't think would be a hit with the Bright family, and toasted cheese sandwiches. She drew in her lower lip and thought for a moment, but before she could answer, Mrs. Bright spoke again.

"You ought to think about ushering as an entry to the work world. You could do it after school, you know," she said. "And on Saturdays."

"There aren't many jobs," said Elizabeth, lowering her head to fight back the tears. She did not want to cry in front of Mrs. Bright, to show how desperate she was. "I really need this one. You see, my father . . ."

"I'm sorry," Mrs. Bright said sadly. Then she pressed a buzzer, thanked her for her time, and the maid appeared at the door. Halfway down the hall Elizabeth smacked her knee on the telephone table, and the maid escorted her the rest of the way, through the parlor and out the front door, with her hand on Elizabeth's elbow.

She stood on the sidewalk with the sun blazing high overhead and a knot of hunger making her even dizzier than the eyeglasses, which she sadly removed. She started walking slowly back down the long, white sidewalk, past the huge houses framed by their wide, green lawns, and dug from her pocket the second-most promising ad. It read:

> 20 additional girls needed as taxi dancers at Fair. Sign-up 18th floor North LaSalle Building Monday 8–5.

She got back on the streetcar and rode all the way up Cottage Grove, over to State Street, and into the Loop. She didn't mind spending a quarter on a hamburger and Coca-Cola in a State Street luncheonette, assuring herself she'd replace it from money she'd be earning.

She walked over to the La Salle building amid the hustling, surging crowds, which swept along the sidewalk like a purposeful army. She was sure they all had jobs, and it felt wonderful to feel, even for a short time, as if she were a part of them. There was only one apple-seller on Van Buren and she hurried quickly past him.

The interviewer was a fat man with a very small head, his black hair slicked down with Vaseline. He didn't say that he was pleased to meet her, just started in with his questions.

"What kind of dancing have you done and how old are you?" He leaned backward in his chair, digging dirt from under a fingernail with a matchbook.

"Seventeen," Elizabeth began. "And I've done all kinds of dancing. In school—"

"Do you always dress like that?" he interrupted crossly. "Like an old maid schoolteacher?"

She shook her head, thinking she ought to explain but feeling suddenly unable to.

"Well . . ." He sighed, and tossed the book of matches onto

the desk. "You don't look like the dancers in New Orleans, I'll say that much. I don't know what I'm going to do. How would you get home from the Fair at night, Cecilia?"

"The streetcar. I'm Elizabeth."

"Tell me about your boyfriend. Is he going to give us trouble?"

"Boyfriend?" she said.

"I see. Well, if you don't have one I guess that's good. I *guess.*" He shook his head as though he were baffled. "Chicago. Nobody warned me."

She asked him about the job. He was vague. She'd charge a fee per dance in the Place du Tertre Cafe and keep a percentage for herself. She thought about how much money that could be but had no idea.

"Place du Tertre, Place du Tertre . . ." She didn't like the way it sounded coming out of his mouth.

She left the building as fast as she could, feeling she'd already done something wrong just by being there and hopped a streetcar right after that, with just enough energy to make it home, up to her room, and into a pair of shorts before anyone saw her.

Elizabeth was certain they hadn't heard her come down the stairs, their voices drifting in from the front porch through the open living room window. It was the tone of her father's voice that nailed her feet to the middle of the living room floor.

". . . and I said I had three kids and a wife to support, and he said, 'I'm sorry, Carl. I hate to cut your hours back but we just can't pay you. . . .' " His voice strained in his throat, like a dog struggling against its collar.

"Maybe I could get something," said Esther.

Her voice was so low, Elizabeth could barely make out what she was saying.

"What? Anything you could get, I could get!"

"I could take in wash."

"Everybody's taking in wash. And nobody's paying. You do enough to save as it is. Who would watch the children?"

Esther sighed. "We'll make it, Carl. I have faith and you should, too."

"John Vanhorn had faith. Up to the last minute, he had faith. Where is he now, Esther? You know where . . . in a shabby basement hole of a place. If I was him, I woulda put a gun to my head. Oh, God . . ."

His words were suddenly muffled, but Elizabeth was sure he was crying.

⇶ 6 ⇜

SHE WENT OUT EARLY EVERY MORNING WITH ADS FOR BABY-
sitters, household help, lamp-shade makers, for hosiery sellers,
waitresses who could also "entertain," and even cigarette girls,
tucked away in her purse. The company that advertised for ex-
perienced colored girls to make buttons wouldn't let her in the
door. She hadn't thought they could *all* be colored.

The kind of job didn't matter. The answer was always the
same. She was too inexperienced, too young; they might give her
a call later. Late every afternoon she came home sweaty and
exhausted, carrying a book from the library because that's where
she'd told her family she was spending her time.

"When are you reading all these books? You're never home
anymore! You're not out with *boys,* are you?" Her father
scratched his stomach through his undershirt.

"I read them at night, Pa. Please pass the corn."

"Uh-huh. You go off every morning; I seen you, all dressed

up to go to the library. What's your daughter turning out to be, Esther? A *tramp?*" He banged the end of his knife on the table. "How would you like a *tramp* for a sister, Waldo?"

Waldo hunched down, his bangs flopping into the corn.

He needs a haircut, Elizabeth thought. She slid her foot forward underneath the table, pressing it against his until he raised his head. She wanted to give him a look that said not to worry. But his eyes were downcast, the sockets hollow and gray.

Elizabeth wiped her forehead, wondering where she could change from shorts into a dress before she got to the streetcar. She didn't want to make her pa more suspicious.

"I bet you'll be glad to get back to school, won't you?" said Esther. "See Vera and your other friends." She looked at her daughter hopefully.

Elizabeth figured her mother wanted reassurance, as though the start of the school year meant that everything would go back to normal again. "Yeah, I will," she replied. But she didn't look at her mother when she said it. She didn't want her to know that school was the farthest thing from her mind. She wished it didn't have to be, that she could go back to worrying about what to wear on the first day and which lunch period she'd have.

"Isn't it amazing?" continued Esther. "To think that the summer's almost over. I'll be glad when it cools off a bit myself." She turned to wipe a smear of food off Whitney's pink mouth.

"Hmmph," said Carl. "In Sweden they're in school already. Where they should be."

"Josef Carlsen's gone back." Waldo looked over at his pa and then at Elizabeth. "I heard it from his cousin. His dad took the whole family back with him."

"Smart man," said Carl. "It might be a hard life, but there's food on the table in Sweden. Always." He ran a small piece of bread around the edge of his plate to sop up the gravy. "Why aren't you eating?"

Elizabeth looked at her mother's plate, remembering what Vera had said. There was almost nothing on it again.

"I already ate."

Elizabeth looked at her pa. He frowned and stuffed the bread in his mouth.

"Sure you did." He sat up in his chair, cocking an ear toward the radio. "Listen to that! A scandal at the Fair!" Turning halfway around in his chair, he began to yell at the radio. "Women dancing with their clothes off at the fair. They should shut them clubs down! Can you imagine this, Esther?"

Esther clucked her tongue and blushed. "Goodness," she murmured, her face clouded with steam from her coffee.

"If a daughter of mine ever . . ."

Waldo threw his fork down and bolted from the table.

"You come back here!" Carl shouted after him.

"Carl," pleaded Esther. "You've made Whitney cry." She lifted the child onto her lap and ran her hand over his head, as he stuck his thumb into his mouth and hiccupped.

"He's no good, Esther. You watch. I bet he steals milk from the porches of old ladies! An' *you!*" He turned to Elizabeth and pointed his fork. He lowered his voice but his words hissed menacingly. "You stay away from that Fair, you hear? An' you stay *home* in the daytime. Library like *hell!*"

Just sit here and he'll stop, thought Elizabeth. She pretended to go on eating, pushing the food around on her plate because it gave her something to look at.

"And I want that *ring* back, Esther. How can you be my *vife wit'out a ring!*"

She saw her ma's haggard face crumple like the napkin in Elizabeth's hand. Then Esther rose abruptly, holding Whitney close to her. "Ring!" she seethed. "You wouldn't be eating at all if I hadda kept it." She turned and charged across the living room, with Whitney crying again in her arms.

43

Elizabeth wanted to run after her, tell her everything would be all right. But it would be just another lie, and she was tired of hearing lies and telling them. She turned to face her father instead, the veins in his temples standing out a vivid blue against his red face. For a moment she thought she hated him, and it frightened her. He was dragging them all down with him, drowning in misery and hopelessness like a man thrown overboard.

"*Aach,*" said Carl, slumping into his chair. "It's not worth it."

She pinched the skin on her forearm and held her breath, remembering what she'd overheard him say that time on the porch. "What isn't?"

"Nothing. Nothing is worth all this."

"Pa?"

"What?" His voice was small, thin and distant.

"Are we broke? Like the Vanhorns? Are we going down, too?"

She waited for him to say something but he didn't, his lower lip trembling as he stared at his plate.

"I want to get a job, Pa. Take a year off of school and . . ."

He shook his head but she kept talking anyway. "Listen, Pa, I can make a few bucks. I know I can get something. . . ." He kept shaking his head, shaking his head so stubbornly, as if what she said wasn't even worth a reply. Finally she gave up and just sat there, twisting the ends of her napkin over and over.

"No, Elizabeth. I know you mean well, but yer goin' back to school." He rose from the table and left the room.

She went outside to water the garden. There were only a few bean plants left. She couldn't think about what would come next. When she went inside, her mother was back in the kitchen, wiping the table and eating a slice of bread and lard.

She started washing the dishes. They didn't talk much.

Up in her room, she thought about what her father had said. He wouldn't keep her inside. He couldn't have meant it. Besides, he wasn't up early enough to stop her, and too downhearted to care. She would keep looking for work, because she had to do *something*.

She didn't land a job the next day, though, or the one after that. It was the same story everywhere, and by Friday night she was tired from walking and waiting and didn't want to give up her last dime to ride the streetcar. She was just relieved the next day was Saturday, and she wanted to sit in a cool, dark movie theater from morning to night.

The railroad tracks seemed to stretch a hundred miles before her, at least as far as she could see; then they merged into a single, thin line and evaporated into a haze in the distance. Picking her way between the ties on her way home from the theater, she was imagining Katharine Hepburn's face as she piloted her plane to a sure death in *Christopher Strong*, wishing she felt half as steadfast.

She didn't even notice the guy with the bundle on his back leaning against the water tank until she was almost past him. He looked up as she was about to pass by, and nodded.

When she thought about it later, she couldn't say for sure what made her stop and take another look. Curiosity, maybe, or something else she didn't know. She bent down and pretended to retie her shoes, but he looked up from his book and caught her staring. She blushed, but felt as though she wanted to say something.

"Didn't know the trains stopped here," she said.

He stared up at her on the railroad bed. "What?"

"I just didn't know they stopped here, is all."

"Well, they don't always. Sometimes just slow down."

She nodded, standing up again. "Just slow down. Uh-huh."

He tugged at the narrow brim of his cap pulled low over his forehead. He looked to be a head taller than she, maybe more, and lanky—very lanky. Even his face was gaunt.

"Sometimes. And sometimes they do stop," he said.

She felt for the few coins in her pocket, letting them slip through her fingers one by one. "And then you get on, I guess."

"Yes, even when they don't stop, I get on." He ran a finger over his upper lip. "You always walk down the middle of the tracks like that?"

She was surprised to think he'd noticed her and maybe had been watching. "Not always." She stopped to think. "It's habit, from looking for coal." She felt herself redden and looked down at the ground.

He nodded, shifting his position against the water tank. "Well, you just ought to be careful."

"Oh, I am," she said. "It's not like the trains creep up on you."

He smiled. "You like living in Chicago?"

"I've never lived anywhere else." She shrugged, as if it were something she should be embarrassed by. Then she stepped over the rail a few feet toward the water tank. He didn't *look* dangerous, and he carried a *book*. "How do you get on if it's moving?"

"You jog alongside and pull yourself up. Toward the front of the car so you don't get sucked under. Stick around and I'll show you."

"Oh thanks," she said. "I have to get home for dinner." She watched him run his thumb along the inside of his suspender, knowing she ought really to get on home and help out. "Where're you from?"

"Kokomo, Indiana." He smiled, as though there was something funny about that.

"I've heard of it." She inserted the toe of her shoe into a crack in the dry, hard earth, then kicked at the edge of the crevice, the hard dirt crumbling in on itself. "I've always thought it should be in Alaska. Kokomo, Eskimo. And now where're you going?"

"To Cleveland. It's only a two-bit town, you know, but there's more work there than here right now. I thought I could get something because of the Fair, but I guess everyone else thought the same thing."

"Work, you said?" She took a step toward him to make sure she heard what he had to say. She was surprised to hear him talk about work, thinking somebody like that would just beg or eat out of garbage cans. He'd looked all right from several feet away, but closer up he looked scruffy. His clothes were shabby, not too clean, and his dark hair grew long down the back of his neck. Even though his blue eyes were friendly, she didn't want to get any closer. "What kind of work?" she asked.

"There's all kinds. I've done about everything already, and that helps to get you in. You know, experience. I think I'll get something right away in Cleveland. Don't get me wrong about Chicago," he went on, slipping the book into his pack. "I like it, but I didn't have any luck here, and if the bulls catch me they'll lock me up. I was already given a warning."

She supposed he meant cops. Why didn't he just say so? It made her wonder again if she should be talking to him at all. To somebody who'd been "given a warning."

"I don't see why it should be better anywhere else," she said. "It's tough everywhere, isn't it?"

"Sure it's tough," he answered, rubbing his jaw thoughtfully. "It's just some places are *more* tough than others. Like some teachers are tough, but some tougher than others. Know what I mean? It's a matter of timing and luck and asking the right people the right questions about where to go."

47

His talking like that made her nervous; she wasn't sure why. "Well, Cleveland's not far, is it?"

"Nope. Want to come along?" He chuckled, scratching the back of his neck.

She felt herself blush and looked away, shaking her head. "Why don't you just go back home if you can't find work?" She was close enough to see a faint dark strip shadowing his upper lip and figured he was sixteen, maybe seventeen years old.

"Because. I'm old enough to be out on my own. I've got seven brothers and sisters at home. Well, no, that's not right. Two other brothers left before me. Anyway, they don't need me taking up space at the table. Besides, I'll get work. I always do."

She jangled the two nickels in her pocket and then blushed again. Suppose he heard it and thought she should give them to him?

He looked away coughing, with the back of his hand over his mouth. "Don't even think about a handout," he said. "I wouldn't take it."

She looked away, then back. "If I had a job myself, I wouldn't mind helping you out. Well, I might soon be getting one, as a matter of fact."

He lifted his eyebrows in surprise and shifted his weight against the water tank. "Is that right? How do you figure to get a job around here? Connections or what?"

She thought by the look in his eyes that he was laughing inside and didn't believe her. "Yeah. Pullman Company. My father used to work there." And it's only *half* a lie, she assured herself.

He whistled. "George M. Pullman, the railroad baron. How about getting me a berth then? You think you could do that?" He put his hand to his back, pretending to be in pain.

"First or second class?"

48

He laughed. She thought it was a good answer and wished Vera was there to see her on this adventure, matching wits with a stranger, a vagabond, like a clever leading lady.

"You've tried the Fair then?" She jangled the nickels again nervously. "Maybe if you keep trying . . ." When her eyes met his, her words faded away. She shrugged instead. "I might also have a job dancing at the Fair. They said they'd call me."

"I've heard that one about a zillion times."

She watched his thumb as it slid under his suspender, feeling his eyes on her face. She knew right then she'd never get hired as a *dancer*, never get a call. What was wrong with her, that she could even think so?

"I wouldn't have taken you for a dancer, just on first impressions. But then it's not my place to say. What kind of dancing?"

She knew her face glowed like a bright neon sign, lit from her neck up to her forehead. "Just dancing," was all she could manage, and then, "I should be getting back."

He yawned with the back of his hand to his mouth and rubbed his eyes, giving Elizabeth a chance to see he could've put on about forty pounds and still gotten into his clothes. His arms were thin and wiry, bones protruding like little knobs at his wrists and elbows.

She wished she could think of some way to help the poor fellow out. She couldn't imagine not having a place to stay. But what could she do?

"I can't let you stay at our house!" she blurted. "My father wouldn't go for it at all."

He stood up straight and narrowed his eyes. "Who said anything about that? Quit thinking I'm asking you for something. I said I have to catch this train in order to get to Cleveland for a job." He readjusted his pack and she knew she'd said the wrong thing.

Scraping the dirt with her toe, she asked him what it was like going off on his own.

"Well, I could tell you stories. . . ." He licked his lips, savoring the possibility. "In a nutshell, it has its high moments and its low ones, all part of the ball game."

"You can get the low ones anywhere." Then she paused, thinking. "You really believe you can get work, huh? What if you get there and there isn't any, like here? You thought you could work here and you couldn't. Maybe it's that way everywhere and all the jobs are taken." She studied his pack, wondering what was in it. If it was full of food or clothes or books or what. And she suddenly wanted him to say that he was kidding, or lying, that there wasn't work anywhere; he'd only been fooling.

"Sure I can get work. I've worked all over. Toledo, Cleveland, Kansas City, Iowa, Detroit, Virginia. It's a lot being at the right place at the right time. Knowing *when* and where the work is. See?"

"Well, I think there'll soon be work in Chicago," she said, trying to sound hopeful. "My father says things are picking up. But he was having a beer when he said that, and he'd just found a five-dollar bill. Oh, well . . ."

"Five bucks, wow." He shoved his hat back.

"Well, this is funny," said Elizabeth. "I don't know you and here I am telling you what my father said."

"Doesn't seem strange to me. But I see how it could to you. Happens all the time on the road. If you feel like talking, you talk to whoever is there. I guess I've been at it a while."

She stopped scraping at the ground and looked him right in the face. "You think things are picking up or not?"

He shook his head. "I don't think they are yet. I think it's as bad as ever and could even get worse. I'm not a pessimist. I'm the opposite, in fact. I always think the big break is around the next corner. But I'd say that we're in for more trouble, and those in Washington who say we're outta the woods, I'd say that was a lot of you-know-what. My dad's a pig farmer. I grew up shoveling shit and I know it when I hear it."

Elizabeth cringed at the word, pressing her lips together and looking off into the distance. "I don't think they're picking up either." She thought she saw a glimmer of movement out where the tracks met the horizon. "I really don't think they are." She tried to picture him chasing the train, then off to look for work in a strange city. It was a brave thing to do and she suddenly thought he was like Mr. Vanhorn, a hero. Women didn't do such things, she reminded herself, except the ones in the movies and Amelia Earhart.

"Here comes one," he said.

She looked up again. He was right. She heard it and felt a sudden sinking in her stomach, but didn't know why. She didn't want him to go off. Not just yet. "I bet you're hungry," she said.

He took a deep breath and dropped his shoulders slowly. "Yeah, I am. I hope she makes good time so I can get somewhere and get a meal."

"We don't have much ourselves these days. But I might be able to scrape something up."

"Naw, I don't want to take food out of other people's mouths." But she saw he couldn't keep the hopefulness out of his serious blue eyes.

"You'd have to wait till after dinner, after my parents are asleep." She was already thinking there was nothing to take, and what was she doing promising something she didn't have? She could spend a nickel on a few pieces of fruit. But her ma needed it as much as he did, and she was hungry herself.

He fumbled with his pack, rearranging things inside of it. "I

51

guess I could wait. Maybe find a jungle somewhere for the evening. I'm not sure, though. This isn't the Illinois River."

She thought for a moment and then replied, "No, it's not." Across the tracks, the weeds grew taller than five feet. That's all she could come up with. "It's not the Illinois River," she repeated. "How will I find you in the . . . jungle?"

"You wouldn't. I'll come back here at dark and wait. You're going to an awful lot of trouble."

"It's nothing. We've got a little to spare." Easier to think of it as a half-truth, instead of a half-lie.

"You sure? Well, thanks again. My name's Eddie." He stuck out his hand.

"Oh," she said, as she shook it, "mine's Elizabeth." She placed one foot behind her.

He nodded as she backed away, up the slope of gravel to the tracks, and started walking. Once she glanced back over her shoulder. He was resting his long, lean frame against the water tank, with his pack drooping over his shoulder, just as he was when she'd first seen him.

7

"I HEARD YOU," ELIZABETH REPLIED. "YOU SAID THERE WAS A parade down . . ."

"It was a *march,* not a parade. You weren't listening. You don't listen anymore because you're always running. It was a march down Michigan Avenue. Communists and Socialists." Her father glowered at her, then slurped noisily from his bowl of broth. Elizabeth could still smell the soap from his shower, but sweat already was beading his forehead. The night was muggy, heavy with moisture that hadn't yet become rain.

"What kind of parade?" said Waldo, leaning precariously back in his chair.

"Please sit *up,* Waldo," said Elizabeth. "You're going to fall back and smack your head."

Carl put his spoon down, looking defeated. "March," he repeated tiredly. "There is 38 percent unemployment in Chicago. Do you know what that means? It means I'm not the only one not working. This was a silent parade. No banners, no cheers. Just a long line of people walking down the middle of the street. I saw them. It was like a soup line, only it kept moving on and on down Michigan Avenue, like a snake."

"We know you're not the only one not working, Carl," said Esther. "And besides, you are."

The spoon was shaking in Elizabeth's hand. She tried to hold it steady, but that seemed only to make it shake all the more. She set it down beside her bowl. She wasn't hungry. Something felt wrong with her stomach and her head. She wanted to lie down but didn't want to leave the table, either. She was afraid to be alone, because she was afraid of the thoughts that might come to her.

There was a thin, watery broth and biscuits the size of silver dollars, and they were sure to get eaten. She'd made a promise and now she couldn't keep it. She thought how it would sound to her pa. "I'm just going to take some food over to this fellow I met at the tracks." He would lock her in the attic, that's what her father would do. He would raise the roof with his yelling and lock her in her room. Was she not only a liar, but a thief as well? And who knew what else. Her father's words came back to her. "Yer not hanging out with *boys*, are you?" She tried to clear her head by shaking it with her eyes closed.

"Where were they going?" she asked absently.

"Nowhere," said Carl. "Just around and around. They didn't have nowhere to go at all."

Even though she was only half listening, she could see a long brown snake in her mind curling down Michigan Avenue. And then she saw that boy, Eddie, leaning against the water tank, talking about where *he* was going to go, to Cleveland. To Cleveland to work and earn money.

She leaned forward to look at the kitchen clock. It was

54

six-fifteen. The Swedish-American Glee Club was in the middle of its half-hour radio show. Her father would move into the living room for the prize fight at seven, and her ma would sew or read on the sofa.

Waldo turned to his pa. "Why didn't you march? We're poor enough, ain't we?"

"I'm not a Communist," said Carl, scowling back. "And Roosevelt will save the country anyway. You watch. Ain't that right, Esther?"

"Well," said Esther. "I think he will in time—" She broke into a fit of coughing, covering her mouth with her napkin, and gasped for air.

Carl leaned to his left and whacked her twice between the shoulder blades. "There, you all right?" he asked. Esther nodded. *"Ja,"* he nodded back. "Okay. I did see John Vanhorn out there, though."

Elizabeth looked up. She was thinking that maybe her father was right and Roosevelt would soon get the country back to normal. She wanted to think it, wanted with all her heart to believe it, and tried to feel a sense of relief. "He's not a Communist, is he?" she asked. She dipped her spoon into the bowl and concentrated on keeping it steady.

"No, Johannsen was out there, too. He ain't been working longer 'n me. We should all go back to the old country instead. America, hah!" He looked as sour as pickled herring.

"He doesn't mean that," said Esther. "He's fooling around. Carl, please don't talk like that in front of the kids."

"Holy cow," said Waldo, peering into his soup bowl. He lifted something from the broth with his forefinger and thumb and dropped it onto the tablecloth. "The leg of a beetle."

Esther's hand flew to her open mouth.

"Stuck to a piece of carrot," he added, examining the specimen beside his plate. "There's a joint in the leg with a little footlike thing. . . ."

"Enough," said Carl. "Take it to the trash and get back to your seat."

Esther's hand was back in her lap but her eyelid fluttered and twitched. "I washed those carrots," she said.

"That kid," said Carl. "I just don't know."

"It was a Communist beetle," said Waldo, slipping back into his chair. "Marching through my soup. No, swimming, *ja.*"

Elizabeth smiled at her brother. She wanted suddenly to hold him on her lap, to squeeze and tickle him, wrap her arms around his bony shoulders.

"He thinks he's funny. Making jokes about Communism. Heh," said Carl.

Waldo studied the bowl intently, stirring with his spoon. "Heh, heh, I tink der may be more."

Carl was laughing. "That kid." Then he began to sway from side to side with the music, singing along in Swedish.

"Uh-oh, we've lost your father." Esther smiled at her children. "Here, Whitney, give me your spoon and I'll help."

Elizabeth looked up and down the table, smiling herself. She'd almost forgotten the sound of laughter. It was wonderful to hear, and she wanted it never to stop. They'd had enough gloominess. Maybe her pa was right. Roosevelt would do the job. The newspapers said so. She spied the two small biscuits left on a serving plate in the center of the table and thought about Eddie again. If she took the biscuits now, they'd all think she was selfish. But if she left them, they'd get eaten, sure as the "Eight O'clock Gang" would steal their milk.

Waldo was swaying and singing now, too, but making up his own words. "Yah, yah, Sveden, yah, yah, Sveden. Da goot life in Sveden, yah goot!"

Suddenly the radio went dead. They all stopped singing, turned in their chairs, and stared. Then Carl slapped his knees and lifted himself heavily from his chair. "Now what?" He trudged from the dining room to where the radio sat, on a table in the farthest corner of the living room. First he tapped it lightly, then he tilted it forward, trying to examine the rear cavity. He set it back on the table and pulled the chain on the lamp for more light, but nothing happened. He sat back, looking baffled.

"What is it?" Elizabeth asked, twisting in her chair to watch him. She grasped a strand of her hair and wrapped it around two fingers.

"Esther, the electric bill is only a dollar a *month,*" said Carl. He lifted the radio onto his lap and flattened his hands across the top, as though to bless it.

"I know, but I couldn't pay it." Her eyelid fluttering madly, she turned to her children. "Go outside and play, or go up to your rooms."

"Esther." He gingerly moved his hand down the row of knobs on the panel, fingering them one at a time. "*Esther.*"

Bam, bam, bam. Elizabeth started. Several blows jolted the kitchen table. "Stop *kicking,* Waldo," she ordered. She turned to glare at him.

"Turn the radio back on," Waldo demanded. He kicked at the leg of the table again and scowled at her. "Go turn it *on,* Elizabeth."

"Oh, I can do everything," she said. "Sure." But he had leaped from his chair and was plunging toward the kitchen door before she even had finished.

"Oh, the hell with it," said Carl.

She turned back to her father in time to see him grasp the radio at either end. It seemed to rise up out of his hands as though it were weightless, then float across the room like a balloon, before

57

it crash-landed in the center of the floor. Then Carl sat back into the sofa, as though delivered of a great burden.

Her mother came up to her room that night, seating herself on the end of Elizabeth's bed, where the last rays of sunlight bathed her in a reddish-gold glow.

"I had the feeling you'd be up here fretting and I wanted to remind you your father gets paid on Tuesday." She gazed out the window, eyes unfocused.

Elizabeth sat up, stuffing the pillow between her back and the wall. "Tuesday," she repeated, then took a deep breath. "I been looking for work myself, Ma."

"*Work?*" Esther turned a startled gaze back to Elizabeth. "You mean an after-school job?"

"Anything I could get. Ma, don't get upset. How can I think about school with things the way they are? I just keep thinking there's got to be something I can do. . . ."

Esther looked as though she might cry. "I know there's something we ought to be doing but I don't know what it is. But school, Elizabeth. You've got to go."

"*Ma*, how can you worry about school *now?*" She felt her cheeks flood with color, her eyes fill with tears. "All summer I was thinking about Vera, living in that dump. It scared me, them being so poor and everything, and now look at us. . . ." Her voice broke and she turned to stare out the window. "There ought to be *something* people could do. It isn't fair!"

"I know," said Esther, biting her lip. "If it's true God helps those that help themselves, we should be doing a lot better. That's what's so hard, when you know you're doing everything you possibly can, and it stays the same or gets worse. Oh, I came up here to reassure you."

Elizabeth looked at her mother's hands covering her face.

The nails were short now, bitten down to the ends of her fingers. Her ring finger still was bare.

"Waldo came back with a bunch of change he said he had hidden in the handlebar of his bicycle. I wonder where he got it."

"I don't know," Elizabeth answered, but she began to think of all the possibilities with a sinking feeling. "I've heard there are ways to get the electricity back on without paying."

"I know, but that wouldn't be right, would it? That would be like stealing."

"This isn't right, either. Is it our fault all this is happening?"

"I came up here to make you feel better and lookit," her ma said again.

"It's okay, Ma. I don't want you to pretend with me. I'm not ten anymore." She paused, staring at her hands in her lap. "If I ever did something and you couldn't understand why I did it, you would just have to trust me, you know." She lifted her head, and seeing her mother's puzzled expression, went on.

"I mean, I would hope you would trust me. That I was doing the right thing, even if it didn't seem so. I'm not stupid or impulsive or anything like that."

"What is it?" Esther searched Elizabeth's face for a clue.

"It's just . . . it's nothing right now," she replied, shrugging, feeling guilty because in her mind an idea had begun to take shape. "If there's ever cause for you to wonder, though, I just want you to remember what I said."

A train blared its whistle off in the distance. She jumped.

"You can come to me with anything," said Esther, reaching out to cover her daughter's hand with her own.

"I know," Elizabeth nodded. But she knew she couldn't really, because the idea taking shape was one she could hardly think about directly, much less talk about, and that made her feel sad and lonely.

59

"Well . . ." Her mother heaved a sigh.

Elizabeth studied her mother's face, the pattern of fine lines which seemed to have extended and deepened, the dusky half moon under each eye. "Sometimes I wish I was little again, and things were like they used to be."

Esther nodded. "So do I."

"It was easier then, wasn't it? Or do I just think so, because I was a kid?"

"No, it was easier. I worry about Waldo, growing up in times like these."

Elizabeth thought about Waldo and the money again, and the "Eight O'clock Gang," and Eddie, and the broken radio in the middle of the floor downstairs. By now, the light in her room had faded to the color of a copper kettle, and she wondered about the time.

Esther pulled at her lower lip. "I've got to put some curlers in so I look nice for church tomorrow morning." She stood, tightening the unraveled belt around her robe, and moved to the window. She sighed. "You do believe in God, don't you, Elizabeth?"

Elizabeth straightened and leaned toward the window, striving to hear what her mother was saying. "Yes, Ma, I believe in God," she replied softly.

"Good. Before you go to sleep tonight, you ask him for his help. All right? Ask him especially to remember all of us in our time of need. Especially your father."

She still stood at the window, looking out. "If I talk to God, I know I don't have to worry. That's faith."

"John Vanhorn had faith," said Elizabeth. "And the Vanhorns are all good Christians, aren't they? But look what happened." Her hands in her lap were like ice, and trembling.

"Well, I've always thought so. But we don't know the

amount of their faith. Only God does, and he knows best about everything, doesn't he? Just remember, first there was darkness, and then there was light. This is a dark time now, but it will get better. And sleep tight, okay?"

"Y . . . yes, mother." Elizabeth waited for her mother to turn and leave, but she still stood staring out the window. Finally, she came toward Elizabeth and bent and kissed her on the forehead. Elizabeth reached up and hugged her, then let go and turned her face away. She heard the trapdoor close a few moments later.

A light drizzle had begun to fall, and the smell of rain-dampened roses blew in through the window. She sat there for a while, just thinking, her mind going over everything, finally settling on what her ma said about God helping those that help themselves. Then she bent over to put on her shoes, discarding the two-tones with the holes threatening to poke through for her ugly, heavy black ones. She went to her closet for a light jacket and noticed something that had not been there before, a short-sleeved white muslin blouse with padded shoulders. Checking the collar and seeing no label, she knew her mother had made it for the new school year, and couldn't imagine where she'd got the money. "Oh, Mama," she whispered, holding the soft material to her chest before putting it back on the hanger.

She left a note, in case she found the courage to do what she thought was needed, then stuffed an extra shirt and jacket into a small burlap sack. Turning to glance about the things in her room, she remembered the scene from *Queen Christina*, how Garbo had said that, in the future, in her memory, she "would live a great deal in this room."

As she turned toward the trapdoor, she saw a dim, dark, reflection of herself in the mirror. She knew she did not look brave or even that pretty, like Amelia Earhart smiling down at her from the photograph on her wall. But she remembered something else Queen Christina had said, something about having a "voice in our souls" which tells us what to do, and we have to obey it.

Cleveland. It had always sounded like such an ordinary word.

⇉ 8 ⇇

SHE WONDERED, ON HER WAY TO THE TRACKS, IF SHE COULD HAVE made the whole thing up. Invented Eddie, like somebody in Hollywood made up a story. As she got closer to their supposed meeting place, she almost began to run, afraid he wouldn't be there and afraid he would.

She could hardly see him in the dim glare of the small light bulb, but he was there all right, asleep on the ground with his head and left shoulder propped against the water tank.

"Hey, Eddie." She whispered it so as not to frighten him. He started anyway, and reached for his pack.

"It's me, Elizabeth. I'm back," she said quickly. She glanced over both shoulders, like someone might rush out of the darkness to grab her.

He straightened and began to rub his face roughly. "Oh, you," he said, squinting in the glare. "You did come. Out in the rain and all." He saw the bag in her hand and looked away.

"I guess it's stopped now." She stared down at him, not sure if it were just the shadows, or if his cheeks were really so hollow. "There's not much in here," she said, still holding the bag. "Maybe I shouldn't have offered."

"Oh, well," he said, drawing his knees to his chest. "Anything helps." He raised his arms over his head and yawned. "Long ride ahead. So anything helps." He looked at the bag again and swallowed.

She held it out to him, thinking he looked even thinner in the dark. "It's not hot food. It's not much of anything."

"Thanks, really." He placed his hand under the bag, as though testing its weight, then opened it and peered inside. "Apples."

She'd picked them off a neighbor's tree on her way over, as there were only the two small biscuits left from dinner.

"And biscuits, yum. What's this?" He withdrew a half-full canning jar and sniffed at it.

"Stewed prunes." She gazed off to her right, down the track until the two rails blurred together in the starry darkness, maybe only a few blocks away.

"Prunes," he repeated. "Well, I'm not sure. . . ."

"You don't like them."

"No, I do. It's just, being on the train and all . . ."

She stood with her hands in her pockets, sweating in the extra layers of clothing.

". . . no facilities, you know."

"Oh!" she said, startled, raising a hand to her mouth. "I never thought . . ."

"But I'll take them, hey!" he laughed, "and eat them one at a time. Maybe I should just have a bite before I get on. If I ride with nothing on my insides at all, it doesn't feel too good."

"Go ahead." She wished she could have given him something better, a roast beef sandwich with mashed potatoes and gravy.

His hand was big, but his long, thin fingers delicately pulled out a biscuit. Then he stuffed the whole thing into his mouth. She tried not to watch him chew, tapping the ground with her foot, looking up and down the track.

"I really appreciate this, as I already said. You do meet nice people on the road." He pulled a piece of biscuit from between his front teeth. "Seems like people who don't have much to give are the most willing to share what they do have. There was this woman in Baltimore who seemed poor as could be herself, but the folks passing through always stopped at her place for a handout. They called her 'the bread lady,' because she would always have some to give. Some houses, like hers, are marked with X's on the front porches or alongside the walls. It means they're good places for a handout. But I don't do much of that myself." He coughed into his shirtsleeve.

"I didn't think so," she replied.

"You could tell?" He looked pleased and waited for her to say more.

"Sure. You didn't even want to take this." She shifted her weight from foot to foot. "I had to convince you, remember?"

"Yes," he said, scratching the back of his neck. "I usually work, but sometimes, you know, you just can't."

"But mostly you do work?" She was rocking back and forth on her heels now, unable to stand still.

He nodded, watching her. "Worried about your parents finding you gone?"

She nodded in return, the back of her throat constricted and dry.

"You could sit down if you want, but I wouldn't blame you for going. What time you think it is?"

"Maybe ten or eleven." She gazed off to her left this time, searching the blackness for an approaching light.

"Well," he said. "I guess I'm off soon."

"To Cleveland," she said.

"Yep, home of the Indians."

"The what?"

"Baseball, the Cleveland Indians."

"Oh, of course, my pa listens to it on the radio. Our electricity went off tonight, though."

"Couldn't pay it?"

"How'd you know?"

"Not hard to guess."

"Listen." She took a step toward him, leaning forward on her toes. "When you work, what do you do with the money?"

He laughed, and she figured he thought it was a stupid question.

"Live off it. I send a little home, too, when I can. Some guys go hog-wild when they're paid. Not me."

She took a deep breath, wishing she could just say it out loud. Would you take me with you? But she couldn't seem to. Every time she opened her mouth to say it, something else came out.

"I didn't think you'd show up," he said. "I figured I'd wait till the next freight came by and if you weren't here by then, I'd hop it. People don't always do what they say they're gonna, you know. I have found that to be true all over. It's a national phenomenon, or maybe a natural phenomenon, one or the other. So I think your coming is a sign."

She brushed her hair from the side of her face and tried to keep her breathing even and slow. "Maybe a sign to both of us."

"What? I couldn't hear you."

"I said maybe a sign from God."

He laughed and stopped suddenly. "Uh-oh, if you meant it, I'm sorry."

66

"I don't know if I meant it or not."

"You just meet a lot of nuts on the road, that's all. I don't mean like you. You don't seem the type at all." He crossed one foot over the other. A round, ragged hole in his sole glared up at her. "I'll bet it's about ten-forty," he said, as a speck of light about the size of a pinhead appeared in the distance down the track.

"I don't have connections at Pullman," she blurted. "Not any more. And I really need a job myself."

He smiled. "I thought you might be exaggerating a little, but you never know."

"I hate lying."

"Do you think it's lying? I don't. It's pretending. It was as much for yourself as for me, wasn't it?" He rolled the bag shut and sighed. "I could keep eating. Boy, could I keep eating." Drawing his feet in close, he rose to his feet. "I hope she slows enough for me to nail her. Hadn't you better get home?"

"I thought I'd watch you get on." Lies, lies, lies. "I've only seen it in the movies."

"So now I'm a star. I like that."

A hollow whistle blew off in the distance. He cocked his head in its direction, where the speck of light was growing.

Elizabeth looked down the track again, her mind on the big glittery eye getting bigger by the second. The whistle this time was lower in pitch, mournful and beckoning.

Eddie approached the track and put one foot on the rail. "From how this rail's vibrating, she's still going at a pretty good clip, I'd say." His head jutted forward, studying the light, his jaw muscles working and tensing. "But she could be slowing. We'll see. Look, I have to, uh, you know, go before I get on, so would you mind walking a few feet away?"

She felt herself blush and took a few steps backward, then turned toward the tracks, as the freighter's rumbling grew louder, competing with the pounding in her head.

He came out from behind the water tank a minute later and strode right up to her. "Well," he said, "I'm glad I met you and sorry I have to get going. You just take care now and get back home so you don't get in trouble on account of me." He tipped his hat and smiled, but his eyes looked sad and serious, as if there were something more he wanted to say.

The train was so close they could hear the engine chugging away and the click-clacking of iron wheel against rail. Then it came bearing down on them suddenly, huge, its whistle blaring, brakes screaming. Elizabeth took an involuntary step backward away from the track as he took one forward.

"It's not going to stop all the way," he yelled, "but I can catch her." Adjusting the pack on his back, he bent to tighten his shoelaces as the enormous white eye raced past them.

She covered her ears to shut out the din of all that metal on metal, wanting to cover her eyes, too, to erase the sight of the menacing boxcars towering and rocking above them. She didn't want the train to slow at all, just to fly right past like a bullet, promising herself if it kept on going she'd *never* come down to the tracks again.

She felt a nudge on her shoulder. "So long and thanks, Elizabeth. I hope you land a job yourself." He tipped his cap again, headed backward down the track on his heels, then turned and ran, his legs working harder and harder as he looked up at the cars rolling by.

"Bye," she said, but she knew he couldn't hear her. She watched him run, his pack bobbing off his shoulder, and then she started running after him. He glanced over his shoulder toward the water tank but didn't see her and didn't hear her footsteps pounding the ground behind him. Finding the car he wanted, he cut in toward it, reaching up and grabbing a rung, then hoisting himself onto the ladder right up the side, over the big white *O* in Chesapeake and Ohio. Elizabeth started running faster, crying by then, until she was right underneath him. She looked up at the ladder, grabbed hold and pulled herself up, hanging by her hands with her face flat against the hard wood surface of the car, until first one foot and then the other found a rung to bolster her.

When she looked up again, Eddie had disappeared. Like a spider quavering in the wind, she clung to the side of the car, her hair swirling across her face, and then she began to climb until she reached the roof. She lay there flat on her stomach, afraid of being blown off if she sat up. The street signs were flying by—120th, 121st, 122nd. . . . They were heading southeast on their way out of the city. She could look straight out but not down.

She crawled toward the middle of the roof, knowing there had to be a way in somewhere. When she found the square hatch, she also discovered that the lid was a lot heavier than the trapdoor to her room, and she had to sit in order to yank it open. She leaned over and peered inside, but she knew the only thing to do was throw her legs over and ease herself down, which she did, letting go only when she could no longer hang on. It was like dropping down into a bottle of ink.

⇶ 9 ⇷

SHE COULDN'T SEE A THING EXCEPT HIS OUTLINE AGAINST THE front of the car, where a pale rectangle of light shone in through a broken slat in the wall.

"Look," he was saying, "when I said that about Cleveland, well, it's not the same for girls out here. This isn't a Coney Island ride, see. I don't think you know what you're doing! Maybe you seen too many movies. The *Shanghai Express* or something, I don't know."

She gripped her ankle with both hands where she'd dropped to the floor in the center of the car. When she began to cry, he reached over and patted her arm.

"You hurt?"

She shook her head, then wiped her eyes with the back of her sleeve. "I know it's not a movie," she said. "And I didn't want to leave, but it's the only thing left I could think of. I can't stay back there and watch it any more. When I heard you say that about work in Cleveland, I knew right then I had to try it."

"I don't know what to say," said Eddie. "What can you do? At least I'd worked on the farm when I left. You . . . you've probably only done your homework and the dishes. How can I convince you?" He removed his hat and ran his hand through his hair.

"I've worked in the yard, too." She rubbed her ankle, trying to ease the throbbing.

"I just can't believe it, that you ran off like this. Well, you'll have to lie if you're going to try it. You can't tell somebody you've only pulled weeds and done dishes."

"I've *been* lying," she answered.

"How do I know you're not lying now? Maybe you're in some kind of trouble. You're not pregnant, are you?"

She felt him glaring in the darkness. She didn't answer, ashamed he would even suggest it. It seemed like a whole minute before he spoke again.

"Well, are you or not? I don't want to be trapped into something."

"I'm only fifteen!"

"So?" he said. "Boy, are you in for some shocks."

She couldn't think clearly and pressed her fingers to her forehead. Then she stood, sure that she'd misjudged him for another kind of person. She would get on another train and find her own way. The boxcar shimmied, swaying from side to side, then suddenly lurched forward, sending her to her knees. She stood again, teetering on her feet like a drunk. "H . . . how do I get off this thing?"

"Take it easy," he said softly. "I'm just looking after myself. Rule number one on the road."

She took another wobbly step toward the door. "I think I'm going to be sick."

"Oh, no. . . ." He leaped to his feet. "Wait till I slide the thing open."

"If you really want to go back," he said a short time later, "at least wait until daylight. I could help you catch a freighter going the other way and it'd be safer."

His words echoed faintly. She was lying on the floor with her head on her rolled-up jacket. Her thoughts were swaying with the movement of the boxcar, first thinking going ahead was the right thing, then thinking she'd done something awful, must've been crazy out of her mind, and she ought to get back before they found she was missing. She sniffed the air, the inside of the car smelling like the stockyards she'd seen with her father when she was a little girl. She wrinkled her nose and sighed.

"I have to say you've surprised me, taking off like this," Eddie was saying. She heard him stir, a slight rustle of cloth against cloth.

The wheels rattled along the tracks underneath her. What had she done? It seemed that one moment she was in her own room at home, talking to her mother, and the next she was here. She wanted to pinch herself and wake up . . . and yet, somewhere out there ahead of them was Cleveland. She tried to see in her mind what Cleveland might look like. It would be clean and white, with new buildings and sparkling-white sidewalks. She'd do anything, even sweep floors like her father. She'd work a month or two and go back in style.

She'd be thinking about Cleveland one moment, trying to feel hopeful, as if she were doing the right thing, and then her thoughts would flash back to Chicago, to how her parents would feel when they found her missing in the morning, and she couldn't separate herself from their sadness.

The shadows cast by the moonlight changed shape, flickered, and faded to a thin gray-beige the color of oatmeal. When she heard Eddie's regular breathing from against his side of the car, she got up and went to the furthest, darkest corner to relieve herself. Something scurried away as she dropped her trousers, and she didn't want to think about what it could be. When the shadows had finally disappeared, replaced by a pale blush of light filtering in through the cracks, she fell asleep.

When she awoke, the light coming through the slat was a dazzling white rectangle slicing the boxcar neatly in half, she on one side, Eddie on the other. Dust motes danced in the air all around them.

It was Sunday morning, and it was not a dream. She still was being carried away in the belly of a beast, like Jonah in the whale. Rolling onto her side, she eased herself into a sitting position against the side of the car.

"It's going to get hot in here fast, even though we're moving."

She thought he was still asleep, but he was resting on his stomach with a book in front of him, watching her.

"You get any sleep?" he asked.

"A little, I guess."

"Hungry? Want a biscuit?"

"Well, I brought them for you." She dropped her head to her knees, hugging them close to her chest.

"It's your food. I'm not going to sit here and eat in front of you. You're probably the too-nice type. I better teach you a few things if you're going to stick it out. Here." He slid across the car and handed her the bag. "Be sure not to leave scraps, or we'll have company for sure, right in your lap, if you know what I mean."

She held the small, yellow biscuit in her hand, knowing her mother had made it. Then, before she even stopped chewing, she gathered and savored every last crumb down to the size of a pinhead.

⇝ 10 ⇜

ALL THAT MORNING, WHILE SHE LET THE FREIGHT CAR TAKE HER
farther away, she yearned to jump off and head back. She longed
to be on her way to Sunday school with Waldo, not to Cleveland.
Cleveland. What had made her think of such a thing? Then, just
as she'd be ready to get off and turn back, she'd think of her ma's
letter to Mrs. Roosevelt asking for coats. Then she would be
thinking about Cleveland all over again and what might lie ahead
if she stuck it out. Cleveland. It had been such an ordinary word,
but now it was not.

"I was there last April and May and I made out all right with
odd jobs," said Eddie. "But I've since heard of other guys who
got steady work there. That's why I'm going back." He laid aside
his book about baseball. "It's not a boom town or anything. . . . Hell, there is no such thing anymore. But at least it
sounds like things are picking up. Otherwise, it's not that different
from most cities. You'll see when we get there." He picked up his
book and laid it open on his lap.

That was enough to keep her going, to let her imagination take its own course. She saw herself behind a desk in an office with a typewriter and telephone, selling clothes in a store, or in a hospital, carrying trays of food to sick people, maybe going on to be a nurse someday. He no longer tried to talk her out of coming and she was grateful. When the train finally stopped, they slid the door open a crack and stepped to the ground. The sun was hanging over them like a huge ball of fire. Already she felt dirty and thirsty.

"Well, here we are," he said. "Cleveland. Now, if you do exactly as me getting out of this yard, we'll be fine. We shouldn't run into trouble." He had told her stories along the way. How a kid named Billy Weber got caught in the barbed wire fence in a Kansas City yard and "the bulls picked him off it like a fly on tar paper." How he'd seen the shackle marks from leg irons on a kid riding east on the C&O line, and how a pal from Brooklyn lost a foot under a freighter, running from the cops in Atlanta. The stories had swirled around her like a heavy, nauseating vapor. It was the one about the foot that finally broke through her own thoughts about home and Cleveland, and she asked him please to stop.

They crawled through the four-foot gap between freight cars, dashing from one train to the next to get across the yard, then scaled a wooden fence to get to the street.

"Just picked off like a fly on tar paper," repeated Eddie as they went over the top. She shuddered, glad there was no barbed wire.

They headed down the center of a wide, empty street, the steel gray and red brick of factories and warehouses looming above them on either side. Cleveland didn't look much different from Chicago so far. Gradually, as they kept walking, the large buildings gave way to small groceries, smelly cigar shops and taverns, hamburger joints, arcades and butcher shops. The streets narrowed, filled with people leaning against the storefronts and hunched together in little knots on the corners. Trash lined the curb and littered the sidewalks.

She followed Eddie down an unfamiliar street in an unfamiliar city, feeling like a dumb dog following its master, his long, thin legs picking their way among the people like a spindly legged insect. But what else could she do? She'd gone off with him, and right decision or not, now she had to trust him, because he knew his way around. He'd been everywhere, after all, and she was lucky to have found him.

Whack. "Ouch! Oh, I'm sorry," she said.

"Watchit, sister."

The old woman glared as she stepped around her. Elizabeth rubbed her nose furiously to get rid of the rank odor of uncleanliness.

"I always feel better when I see people dirtier 'n me," said Eddie. "I know that's mean."

Elizabeth wondered if she smelled yet herself but felt too timid to ask about washing up. She couldn't imagine where, but she knew he would know.

"I wonder if they can get me for kidnapping," he said. "You know, like the guy who stole Lindbergh's baby. Heh." He smiled.

"I came on my own."

"And you're not a baby. It was just a joke, Elizabeth. I've never met anyone so serious. Are you worrying about your parents? They'll be all right. It's just hard at first. You can write to them, you know."

"Well, it's just for a short while, anyway," she said, turning to look up at him. "I'm not *moving* here or anything. Just going to help them catch up. I'm not leaving for good like you did. I would never do that. . . ." She tried to slow her ragged breathing.

"Yeah," he said, jutting his chin out and looking straight ahead. "All right."

They stepped past a prone figure face down on the sidewalk, and she shuddered. What if the person was dead or dying? If there *were* people out of work in Cleveland, they ought to at least get them off the sidewalk. She imagined the train must've left them off in the worst part of town.

"Poor sucker," said Eddie, shaking his head. "I remember how it was when I first left. That lost feeling because you don't belong anywhere and you don't know where you're going. The cold feels colder and your empty stomach feels emptier. It's a lot better if you have someone to go around with. I learned that fast."

She understood how he must've felt, but he seemed so self-assured, she almost couldn't picture him lonely. But she did belong somewhere, she assured herself, and what's more, she'd already reached her destination. They were here already, in Cleveland. She glanced up and down the street and then up at Eddie, realizing she still had no idea where they were headed. "Where're we going?" she finally asked. She thought something ought to happen right away, now that they were in Cleveland.

He thought for a moment, rubbing his chin with his forefinger, and then cleared his throat. "Well, I'm hungry and I'm sure you are, too, so I think we ought to grab a bite to eat."

"Yes," she said with relief, "let's." But his face told her nothing about where they would eat or what. She'd left home with only ten cents and hoped to hang onto it until she was working, so she was glad once again that he knew what to do, even if he wasn't talking.

A short time later, he stopped in the middle of the sidewalk and pointed ahead to a line of people streaming down the block and around the corner. "There's some place we could eat," he said, with a hint of hesitation.

She squinted into the sun. The inside of her stomach was like an empty cavern. She knew he was right about eating. They ought to, and she was hungry. But she'd been afraid to ask him where and what they would eat, and now she knew why. "Oh, no," she replied.

He took hold of her elbow. "C'mon, let's go see."

Reluctantly, she let herself be guided along until they fell in behind some young boys at the end of the line. The boys had turned and were laughing. They looked ignorant and stupid and told Eddie a joke and punched him on the shoulder as if they were his old, best friends. When the bony, redheaded one opened his mouth, she saw a black space where a tooth should have been, and she swallowed, studying the tops of her shoes. It was only temporary, she reminded herself and searched the line ahead for other girls. There were only a few, far as she could tell.

It was an hour before the "snake" began to creep forward. Two steps forward and stop, two forward and stop. It wound its way around the corner past an old black pickup like the one that had hauled Vera away. In the back of the truck, a boy in a blue suit and a girl in a matching blue dress were playing an upright piano and singing "The Old Rugged Cross." Hung from the side of the truck was a crudely hand-lettered sign:

JESUS SAVES
YE MUST BE BORN AGAIN!

Her eyes filled with tears, Elizabeth felt both lifted up by the familiar hymn and ashamed, as though she had fallen out of God's favor. "I don't want to go inside," she said, drying her eyes on her shirtsleeves.

Eddie stopped whistling to look at her solemnly. "Why?"

"I don't want to eat in there. . . ."

"We've got to eat *some*where. First things first. It won't

always be like this, but you can't look for work on an empty stomach."

"With all th . . . those people. . . ."

"Huh," he said, hunching up his shoulders. "Suit yourself. I wouldn't either, if I had a choice."

The boy without the tooth turned, blinking up at her. "Hey, look, it ain't bad here, girlie. No bugs or nothing."

When they reached the front entrance, people straggled past them on their way out. Some carried sacks and others toted children. Several had no shoes, and she saw one man whose bare toes poked out from under his shoe tops like clown feet. She couldn't seem to keep herself from staring.

The smell inside was revolting, like bleach and tobacco and pee. There wasn't much talking, mostly the scraping of the metal chair legs on the tile floor. As she thrust a tin plate forward, she was sure that what was happening to her couldn't be real.

"Bless you, sister." The man's silver cross dangled from his neck over a huge, steaming pot as he dipped down for a ladle of beans and dumped it onto her plate. A woman next to him dropped a slice of bread next to the beans.

"Think of it as a church potluck," said Eddie, leading the way across the room to two empty chairs at a long, metal table. "It's the same kinda thing, really." He set his tray on the table. She set hers next to him and sat down.

"That's a good one, son. Original." A middle-aged man in a threadbare suit looked up from across the table. "I wish it *was* a church thing. Then when we were done eating, we could play bingo." He shoved a spoon of stew into his mouth and opened it again. "G-54, N-27 . . ."

Elizabeth looked down at her food. The beans had fanned out into a wide pool across her plate, drenching her bread. She had been so hungry.

"Eat," Eddie was saying, scooping his food up hungrily. "I

79

think there are bits of ham or something mixed in. Army surplus. Just watch the color. Pink or red meat is okay. Green or yellow is not."

Elizabeth picked up her fork and took a deep breath. A small boy next to her was singing to himself as he stirred his beans. "Pink and yellow, green and red, red and yellow, and purple and blue. . . ."

"Say, Henry."

Elizabeth heard a voice from behind her.

"I heard the cook lost his cat in the kitchen this morning. He can't find it anywhere. You don't suppose . . ."

She threw her legs over the bench and ran toward the door.

"Hey!" Eddie called after her, "Elizabeth!"

When she pushed her way out through the doors of the mission, she saw that the line still curled halfway down the block. Trembling, she leaned against the front of the building, not sure what to do. Nobody was paying attention to the boy reading the Bible, as he waved his arms and ranted, his hair dripping with sweat. The girl playing the piano softly behind him, her fingers gliding over the keys without effort, reminded Elizabeth of how they did the "call to come forward" at Vera's church. She and Vera had "gone forward" once together when they were about twelve, gripping each other's hands as they went down the aisle in tears.

The girl looked over at Elizabeth and smiled. She found herself smiling back, despite the boy's reading about the fires of hell, and she stepped a few feet forward. Maybe the girl wanted to talk. Maybe they had something in common. She stood near the rear of the truck for several minutes, and then the girl leaned toward her. Elizabeth looked up, waiting and smiling. "God loves you," said the girl. Then, seeing what she must look like through the girl's eyes, her smile faded as she backed away toward the

80

corner. When the light changed she crossed the street and stopped, not knowing where to go. Leaning against the window of a magazine shop, she closed her eyes and longed for her mother.

"Next time give *me* your plate," said Eddie, shaking his head as he approached her. "It's an old trick the bums use, you know, to get extra food. I never saw it work better before, though. I should've warned you. Anyway, let's get going."

She began to follow him down the street, feeling like a dumb dog all over again, this time one that had been scolded. She pulled her hair back and twisted it, trying to keep it out of her face, but it fell forward again in front of her eyes. Instead of one glaring white-hot sun, there seemed to be hundreds—reflecting off the cement sidewalk, glinting from store windows, off automobiles passing by.

She could barely lift her feet, while he sprang along as if he hadn't a care in the world. He seemed so young just then, and for a moment she doubted he *did* know what he was doing. Perhaps it had been a mistake, and she should let him go on alone. But then what? She didn't even know the way back to the railroad yard.

He slowed and glanced at her. "I know that wasn't much of a Sunday dinner."

She didn't say anything, just stared ahead, and then he took her elbow again and steered her down a side street toward a small park with half a dozen or so trees and two benches. She felt a sudden spurt of hope. It looked more like the Cleveland she'd imagined.

"Let's just take a break then," he said, tossing his pack down. She sat down beside him on the grass as he placed the pack between his knees. He dug down into it and extracted two slices of bread. "I made them give me back the bread at least." He smiled at her warmly, and laid a slice of bread on her left knee, and then one on her right.

She stared at the bread and smiled back at him shyly. "You've given me two pieces," she said. "So one must be yours." She took the piece off her left knee. "Here, Eddie, take yours back. I only want one." She held the bread out in her open hand, but he lay back in the grass with his eyes closed.

"Here, Eddie, c'mon." She nudged him on the shoulder.

He lifted his head and slipped the canteen from his pack. Then he sat up and reached for the bread, pulling off a corner piece about the size of the end of his thumb. He put the canteen to his lips and drank, then ate the piece of bread. "There," he said, looking satisfied and happy. "I've had Communion. Now I don't feel so guilty."

"Guilty for what?" she asked. But he'd turned his head and shut his eyes.

The park was quiet, the grass soft, and she wanted to know why they couldn't stay there until morning. Eddie said it would increase their chances of getting picked up. "Besides," he added, "we might get a tip about work."

They walked back to the mission a few hours later to stand in line for bed space. The sidewalk seemed hot enough to melt the soles of her shoes. She didn't see how those without shoes, or without soles on their shoes, could stand it. When they got to the front of the line, the mission worker sent Elizabeth in one direction and Eddie in another. "Sleep tight," he said, waving.

She was glad he didn't finish the saying.

"That your boyfriend?" asked the girl following her into a small, bare room.

Elizabeth shook her head.

"He's cute. I'll take him, then."

It seemed there was only space for about twenty people, but there were more than thirty females jammed together in rows on the hard, tile floor. Elizabeth wasn't sure whether to cover herself with the blanket she'd been given or use it as a cushion underneath her body.

A small knot of girls were whispering and smoking off in a corner, tossing the butts on the floor in spite of the NO SMOKING signs. They were the kind of girls always in trouble in school, the kind she would have stayed away from. Elizabeth rolled onto her side. She hadn't noticed the colored person next to her until then and didn't want to stare, but she was surprised to see how light the palms of the woman's hands were, which she had curled beneath her head.

She thought about home before she fell asleep and saw the faces of her family, one by one. Maybe they were now more troubled than ever, had called the police. . . . She raised the blanket over her head, as though it would stop her from thinking.

When she awoke the colored woman next to her had already gone. Elizabeth sat up and folded the blanket into a neat square. Her hair was a tangled mess. She didn't have a comb, or a toothbrush, or anything to wash up with. After handing in the blanket, she went off to find the bathroom, where the same girls were smoking and giving each other haircuts.

She ran her fingers through her own messy hair in front of the mirror, casting a sideways glance at the tough girls.

"Watcha looking at?" The cigarette trembled on the girl's bottom lip.

Elizabeth turned and leaned against the sink, feeling flushed all over. "Could I cut mine, too?" she blurted.

They poked each other and laughed. "Oh, well," said one. It was the girl who'd asked her about Eddie. "Why not? Have to wait your turn, though."

She watched, as clump after clump of hair fell to the floor. Then they handed her a comb and scissors. She snipped off a piece just below her earlobe, then cut the rest as quickly and evenly as she could, the loose strands falling like little sticks in a circle around her feet.

"Oh, God," someone said. "You've hacked it to pieces in the back." Grabbing the scissors from her hand, the girl went to work on it herself. "Hold still so I don't stab your neck. I'm shaking from all the smokes." They clustered around her, telling their friend where to even it out, where to snip a little more.

"Well, now the back is shorter then the front. I'll have to take a little more there." She cut another inch in front and stepped back to look.

Elizabeth backed away from the mirror, not finding the face with the short, straight hair either familiar or attractive. She thanked them anyway, on her way out turning to ask, "Where do you suppose I could get a job here in Cleveland?"

They laughed harder this time and looked at her as if she were crazy.

She stood on the front steps, looking down at Eddie. He stared right past her, then blinked.

"Thought maybe you left without me," he said. "That is a haircut, isn't it? Well, let's see."

She ran her hand through it, fingering the blunt ends just below her earlobe. "It's like it was sawed off, isn't it? Never mind. I don't want you to say anything."

He chewed his lip as though to keep from smiling, thrusting his hands deep into his pockets.

They hitched the six blocks over to the mission mess hall for coffee and bread. It was Labor Day, September 4, but that didn't mean much to her, except that they couldn't look for work on a holiday.

⇢≫ 11 ≪⇠

THE RAILROAD GUARDS IN CLEVELAND STOOD IN A LINE TO KEEP them from getting on the train until it was moving. *Whap, whap, whap.* They slapped their clubs into their palms like tough-guy cops in the movies. Elizabeth thought of the firing squad in *Mata Hari* and tried not to look back at them, peering over a dozen heads at the hulking, stationary C&O freighter.

"You heard what everybody's been saying," Eddie had told her the night before. "There's no work here anymore. It's no better than Chicago. Look, I'm sorry. I woulda told you if I'd known."

He said he had a new lead from a reliable source he'd met at the mission. Pittsburgh was the place to go, and they'd be getting a jump on everyone else if they went now. They couldn't lose, far as he could see.

She'd thought about it all night long, knowing he might be right and she wouldn't know any better if he were wrong. Pittsburgh. It sounded like Boston and New York and those other eastern cities, so far from Chicago. But they'd spent days combing the streets, the ads, the employment offices, looking for work, and there was nothing. It wasn't Chicago all over again, it was worse. Who would hire her looking the way she did? She washed up in a sink at the mission, then another time in the ladies' room in a bus depot. But she never felt clean, and she always felt hungry. Several times each day she decided to give up and go home. But she couldn't seem to get on a train that would take her back. She couldn't get on alone. She'd seen too much in six days to want to go anywhere alone. She wanted to ask Eddie to take her back, but she was ashamed. He was still so sure they'd get something. He'd worked all over, after all. He'd earned real money. She saw her parents opening an envelope, with money inside that she'd sent. She would just hang on a while longer. She remembered what her mother had said, that darkness always came before the light. There was always the darkness inside the railroad car, then the sun blazing overhead when they'd drop to the ground. Nothing stayed the same forever.

He'd shown her his map. "See. Pittsburgh's the next town over, only Akron in between." So he'd been wrong about Cleveland. That didn't make him a liar. Anybody could make a mistake, and he seemed as disappointed as she was.

Whap, whap, whap.

She bit her lip and looked around at the restless, swelling crowd waiting for a signal. She was just part of a herd now. Eddie had been right about one thing, the guards not letting them on in Cleveland until the train was moving. He'd said every city was peculiar in its own way. "Take Atlanta. You only go there on your way to somewhere else. They like to round up the tramps and put them in chain gangs." She wondered if he liked to exaggerate, to make his life sound more exciting.

"There'll be a lot of shoving and pushing, but we won't try

for the same car as everyone else," he'd said. "And most people won't give you the elbow." *Give you the elbow,* she thought, staring straight ahead. The guy next to her had forearms like a prizefighter.

"If they do, give it back to them harder, show you can hold your own." Sure, Eddie, sure. She sighed, keeping her eyes on the flat, broad side of a boxcar directly behind an open coal car, avoiding the massive, steel gray structure of wheels underneath.

A spray of steam hissed up from the engine. She drew in her breath. The guards stepped forward, still tapping their clubs until the fireman rang the bell. The train jerked, rumbled, and started rolling. The crowd pushed and surged, scrambled up the sides of the cars and onto the roofs, or jogged alongside until they were able to slide open a door. A child fell, wailed, and a woman scooped it off the ground and ran for an open car.

Elizabeth and Eddie hoisted themselves up a ladder to the roof, just as the freighter was picking up speed. Elizabeth recoiled from a blast of stale heat as she lifted the door, then began to lower herself over the side.

"Just a minute, hold on," said Eddie, pulling her back. "Always stick your nose in first." He leaned over the opening and sniffed. "Okay, go ahead."

She dangled by her hands for a minute before dropping to the floor and crawled away quickly to give him space.

"Once I rode for seven hours on top of a pile of fertilizer." It was just his voice, which sounded deeper in the dark beside her. "It was comfortable, like somebody's soft stomach, but then I had to throw everything out and start over. Didn't want to smell like a polecat."

She slid across the floor until her back was up against a wall. The freighter was picking up speed, the *click-clacking* underneath coming faster and faster.

"Another time I rode from Tallahassee to New Orleans with a crazy man who thought I was his dead brother come back to get some money he owed him. 'Walker, I swear I don't have it!' he yelled at me over and over. When I tried to leave he hung onto my sleeve and bawled his head off, saying how sorry he was. Took me a while to ditch him in New Orleans. Know how I finally did it?"

"How?" she asked, wondering if he was going to tell stories the whole way to Pittsburgh. She didn't mind them so much really, as long as they weren't about tramps getting run over by freight cars.

"I sent him over to this garden to pick vegetables. Said I knew the family who owned it. They chased him away and I ran in the other direction."

"That seems kind of mean," she said absently. "I mean, being crazy, maybe he needed some help." She hated the dark and wished there were windows, as in a passenger train, a Pullman. Maybe soon they'd be out of the city and then they could slide open the door. Pittsburgh, Pittsburgh. All she could see was a smokestack.

"Sure he did," said Eddie. "But *I* couldn't help him. Now, don't go thinking I'm going to ditch you. This was different. I thought the guy might try to knock me off. It happens."

"I wasn't thinking that," she answered. But then she did. She saw just how it would happen, how she would end up alone with just the clothes she wore, standing beside a black smokestack. She slid along the wall closer to Eddie.

She'd spent her last nickel on a couple of oranges, choosing the oranges over a postcard home. What would she have said to them anyway? She pulled an orange from her pocket and bit into it, puckering her lips at the tartness of the rind. "How long then to Pittsburgh?"

"Not long at all. We can make it today if we ride straight through. That is, if she doesn't fool us and pull into a yard somewhere. Or just sit in the middle of a field, which is worse, since you can't often get another train unless you want to go back the way you came. Sometimes I think they like to do that when they know they're carrying a full load of people. . . . Can we split that orange now and the other one later?"

Elizabeth handed it over. The freighter rocked them gently back and forth, like a giant cradle. She'd had a decent night's sleep in a Catholic church basement the night before, but the previous night they'd had to sleep in someone's yard, and she hadn't slept much at all. The church gave them stew, bread and coffee, and more bread for breakfast. But she was hungry again. She liked oranges because they both quenched her thirst and filled her stomach, but they didn't stick with you for long.

He held the orange in the palm of one hand and sliced it in half with the other. After licking the juice from the blade of his knife, he wiped the edge on his pants leg and handed her half. "We could've stayed in Cleveland forever and not got a thing," he said again. "You saw how it was."

"Tell me again. What kind of jobs do you think we might get in Pittsburgh?" She could see his outline but only dimly make out his features.

"Well, there are the steel mills for one thing. Some have been on strike, though, and we don't want to get messed up crossing a picket line, not even for a job. It's a big manufacturing city, see, and I don't think we'll have much trouble. There's the coal mines, too, but they don't hire girls. But, like I said, there's all that manufacturing. . . ."

"Nothing's happening in Pittsburgh."

Elizabeth's head snapped up. She turned her face toward the other end of the car, where the words had come from, as her mouth went dry, and her breath came shallow and ragged. Eddie reached for the knife resting on his thigh.

"Take it easy, mister. I'm not about to *shoot* you. I'm just telling you something you ought to know."

"Yeaaah?" said Eddie slowly, as if he didn't know what else to say and was buying some time to think.

"Well, you seem to know a lot already," the voice drummed on, "so maybe you already knew this, too. Pittsburgh is dry and dead as wood. I'm sorry to bring you bad news. I almost laughed when I heard you, though. I thought at first you were making a joke about all those steel mills. Ha! . . . ."

Elizabeth tried to breathe slowly, but the air seemed thick and heavy, not even breathable.

"How do *you* know so much?" asked Eddie, his voice tight and raspy. "If you're on your way to Pittsburgh, how do you already know it's so bad?"

"I was tryin' to be helpful. You can go there if you want. But why do you s'pose there's a herd leaving Cleveland? You'll have to go further than Pittsburgh."

"Eddie, let's go." Elizabeth pulled at his shirtsleeve.

"You can leave if you want," said the stranger. "I'm not going to hurt you or anything. But I'd get this boy to tell you the truth. Before he gets you to Hong Kong, looking for work."

"Why are you hiding?" asked Eddie. "I don't like talking to someone I can't even see. Makes me real nervous."

"*C'mon*, let's go." Elizabeth sat cross-legged, rocking back and forth.

"I'm not hiding," the stranger declared. "Not that you'll see me much better up close." Scraping and sliding across the boxcar floor, the entity took shape as it drew closer. It was long and dark with a big head, but no face. It had eyes, though, and teeth.

"Eddie, *c'mon.*"

The person was colored, its colored face about two shades lighter than darkness. The shape was a girl or woman's but she seemed to have no hair.

"It's none of my business," the woman said more softly, "but you ought to take her past Pittsburgh if you both want to work. It's fall, harvest time for some folks. I've done a little work outside myself and it's not bad if the farmers are decent."

Elizabeth could feel the woman's eyes scouring first Eddie, then her.

"I guess you've worked in the fields yourself," she said to Eddie.

"I grew up in them."

"Potato head."

"What?"

"I said you're lucky. I'm from New York, but I can't say I'll ever go back."

"Why not?" he asked.

"Running from the cops. Shot my boyfriend in the head."

Elizabeth's own head pounded. She drew in her breath.

"Ha!" the woman laughed, showing her teeth. "Gotcha! But that was mean. I didn't do any such thing."

"That was real funny," said Eddie. He cleared his throat. "You get on back at the yard?"

"Yes, I did."

"Oh," he said, "we were hoping to ride alone."

"So was I," said the colored woman, "but here we are." She held out her hands and then let them drop, a gesture that seemed to say, "We'll have to make the best of it."

"We could flip for the car," said Eddie.

"You got something to flip?" asked the woman.

He looked at Elizabeth. "You got any more?"

She shook her head.

91

"I didn't think so. You the 'sugar mama'?" the woman said, laughing.

"Oh, God," said Eddie. "Sure."

"My name's Lenora. One thing being on the road does. It helps you get over being shy." She untied a pillow case and unwrapped a small, rectangular object. "If you're hungry, I don't mind sharing."

Elizabeth looked at what she thought was probably a hunk of bread in the woman's outstretched hand, then up at Eddie's face. She imagined his face the same color as the bread, a pasty white.

→» 12 «←

"SHE'S NOT QUITE RIGHT, DO YOU THINK?" EDDIE LEANED TO-ward Elizabeth, his fingers cupped around his mouth. She could still smell the orange on his hand, though several hours had passed since they'd eaten it.

She did not want to think that the woman wasn't "quite right," because she didn't want to be riding along inside a dark, gloomy freighter twenty feet away from someone who wasn't.

Eddie nudged her with his elbow. "Oh," she answered. "Maybe she's lonely or something." But Lenora had retreated to her end of the car and stayed there since they'd eaten the bread. Swallowed up like Jonah.

"I've ridden with colored people before," he whispered. "It's not that. Well, don't worry. We'll get off in Pittsburgh, anyway."

She didn't like even the hint of concern in his voice, still wanting him to know everything, have all the right answers. He'd done this before, after all.

"I don't want to go to Hong Kong," she said.

He wiped his mouth and kept his voice low. "Look, I don't think she is quite right, so she can't know what she's talking about. I say we don't listen to her and go ahead with our plans. You don't want to work on a farm, do you? I mean, you don't make much money."

"Then, no, but there are an awful lot of us headed for Pittsburgh." She thought about Cleveland again and how he'd been wrong.

"Sure, but think of all the ones left behind," he was saying. "Look at all the people back in Chicago and Cleveland. Hundreds of thousands of them, and *they're* not going to Pittsburgh."

The freight car lurched forward with a jolt and then smacked to a stop, throwing her hard against his shoulder. "Ouch!" she cried, holding her jaw.

"Derail," came the woman's voice out of the darkness.

"Nah," said Eddie. He sat back up and tapped Elizabeth on the knee. "You okay? Just some cattle on the track, is all." He stood and went to the door, heaving his shoulder against it until it slid open enough to let him through. Not wanting to be inside with just Lenora, Elizabeth rose and dusted her hands off, then followed him across the car. He hadn't even waited for an answer. She rubbed her jaw again and fingered her lip, suddenly aware of the taste of blood in her mouth. Poking her head out, she smelled something acrid, like burning metal.

"Cattle, bull," said Lenora, and she snickered.

Elizabeth jumped, flexing her knees as she hit the cinders with both feet. Eddie had gone ahead to look. As she stepped out away from the car, she could see something down over the side of the tracks ahead. Other people had jumped out of their boxcars and were walking along the rails or standing and talking in little groups. She leaned over and spat some blood into the cinders.

"It's good to see the sun again, isn't it?"

Elizabeth looked up. Lenora towered in the doorway, shielding her eyes. "Yeah, yeah, it is," she said. She saw that the woman wasn't bald, only had her head wrapped in a scarf.

"I think we're past Pittsburgh."

"*Past* it? I think Eddie would've said so."

"If he had known."

Elizabeth took a step down the track away from Lenora, afraid something crazy would come out of her mouth and she'd know for sure.

Lenora raised her arms until they touched the top of the doorway and yawned, her mouth a gaping hole, which she didn't try to cover. Elizabeth noticed she had a tear in her blouse, underneath her arm.

"He your boyfriend?" she asked.

"No, no, he's not."

"He's kind of a wild one, ain't he?"

"What do you mean?" She was startled and couldn't help staring up at her.

"Oh, just a feeling I get. Like he's done a lot of living for a boy. Kind you got to be careful with. I guess it's none of my business." She scratched under her arm and laughed. "You know, the kind that's always got an angle."

She vaguely knew what Lenora was talking about and wanted to walk away. Eddie was striding back down the cinders toward them with another boy, whose arm hung limply in a red bandanna sling.

"You haven't been on the road long," said Lenora.

"No. Just since Chicago."

"Yeah? Been to that big Fair?"

"No." She kicked a cinder, wishing Eddie would hurry along.

"Here comes that boyfriend. I wonder what you'll do. Go back or what?"

She was glad Eddie was back, taking a step toward him and wiping her mouth.

"This here is Tony," he said. "And this is Elizabeth." He squinted up into the freighter's doorway. "And up there is Leona."

Elizabeth nodded shyly, wondering why he brought a stranger back to meet them.

"It's *Lenora*. They get the cows off the track?"

"Here's the deal," said Eddie, ignoring her. "Tony says we should start walking ahead to the next town, not wait for this train to get going again. He says he knows where there's work, and it's not around here. It's farther south, and we could catch another freighter going that way up ahead. Whaddya say?" He anchored his thumb in a suspender and stood waiting, watching Elizabeth's face.

Elizabeth stared back at Eddie in shock. She could see he wasn't kidding, that he meant to take them farther away once again. "What about *Pittsburgh?*" she asked, trying to keep her voice steady.

"Well, actually, we've gone a little past Pittsburgh. I don't know why she didn't stop there. She always does." He shrugged to show it wasn't his fault.

Elizabeth felt as though something had come loose and slipped down inside her, that it was falling all the way to the pit of her stomach. *Past Pittsburgh.* How could that be? Maybe he *was* a liar, or stupid, and she should really be afraid. She looked at the cars down on the track ahead, rolled over onto their sides like crippled horses.

"How far past Pittsburgh?" she asked, probing his face because of what Lenora had said.

"Not too far," Tony offered. "Half hour's ride back. But we're all going to walk up ahead to the next town to hitch a ride south. The farmers are crying for help in Virginia. You're all free to tag along."

"Virginia?" Elizabeth laughed drily. She felt a line of perspiration trickling down the side of her forehead. "Well, I'm going back to Pittsburgh myself."

"Oh," said Eddie, "sure." He turned to Tony and smiled, hitching up his pants. "She's walking back to Pittsburgh. By herself." The kid smiled vacantly back.

"You said we could get something in Cleveland," said Elizabeth. "We didn't. Then you said we'd get something for *sure* in Pittsburgh. . . ."

"All that manufacturing," Lenora cut in.

"That's really smart," said Eddie. "A girl alone out walking in the middle of nowhere. Look around. Who's going to hear your cry for help?" He stood with his fists on his hips.

"Who's going to make her cry?" asked Lenora. "There isn't anyone out here but us."

He glanced at her and spat on the hard, gray ground.

"I don't want to go to Hong Kong, Eddie. I just wanted a job in Cleveland." Whatever it was that had slipped down inside her had risen again and sent her spinning on her heels. She began to head west along the cinders. If she couldn't get anything in Pittsburgh, she'd just head home, admit it had been a mistake. She kicked at a stone and wiped her eyes. The black cinder dust swirled up into her nostrils. She'd go back to the Fair. See that guy again about the dancing job. Do anything. There had to be *some*thing. The thought of Chicago made her start to walk faster. Her feet felt lighter; even her head felt lighter.

"Hey, Elizabeth."

She didn't want anybody to stop her, talk her out of it.

"Yoo-hoo, girl. Some water!"

It was that colored woman's voice and she turned reluctantly because she couldn't be downright rude, not even to her.

Lenora was striding alongside the track, holding her skirt up with one hand and a jar in the other. "Here's some water if you want it," she said when she had caught up to Elizabeth. "But your friend's right and I'm not. Somebody could pop out of one of these cars and drag you off. . . . How old are you?"

Elizabeth turned to the west again, looking beyond the long stretch of train, which wound around to the left until it was out of sight. "Fifteen." She didn't like telling this Lenora anything. She was fifteen, and she was supposed to be in school. What day was it? What *state* was she in?

"You could walk ahead with the others, catch a train back when it comes by later. Don't go by yourself. Don't go back alone."

It wasn't so much the words themselves; it was how she spoke them and the entreating gesture of the woman's hand beckoning her to return. They seemed to nail Elizabeth's feet to the ground, and she couldn't take another step forward.

"Have some water," said Lenora. She unscrewed the cap and held out the jug.

Elizabeth took it and drank. They walked back along the track together, engulfed in the cool shadows of the boxcars.

Eddie shook his head, his mouth a tight, even line, when he saw her coming, as if she had been a silly, foolish child. "She'll go back later," said Lenora, as though Elizabeth had lost the power to speak.

→⟫ 13 ⟪←

THE TRAIN HAD DERAILED IN A CORNFIELD, CHUNKS OF COAL CAS-
cading like a sea of black jewels down to where the corn grew in
straight, tall rows. Two empty cattle cars also sat askew of the rail,
the underside of one resting on the track like a huge, beached
whale. Two train crew members stood gazing up at it, its front
end dangling up off the ground, tilted toward a steel blue Pennsyl-
vania sky.

Elizabeth hung toward the rear of the small group straggling
along the passageway between the rows of crops and the crippled
C&O. Ahead of them, in small clearings down off the track, two
fires already were blazing. They passed three men dismantling an
abandoned shack by hand, tearing and kicking at the rotten wood.

Her mouth tasted of coal dust, dry as chalk. She could smell
it and taste it and feel it in the grittiness of her skin, a fine powder
on her eyelids and in the corners of her eyes.

Lenora walked just ahead of her, and ahead of Lenora were
Eddie, the boy with the sling, and his friends.

Some older men had a fire blazing and invited them to roast the corn they'd picked, which crackled and sizzled after they threw it in. The smell made Elizabeth remember how hungry she was. Soon, empty corn husks and strips of corn silk ringed the circle, littered about everyone's feet like discarded holiday wrappings at a Christmas party. The remains of the shack were stacked in the center near the fire. Every so often somebody got up and threw a piece on.

Elizabeth looked at Eddie across the circle, picking his teeth with a matchstick. She felt confused again and afraid. What if he were mad that she'd almost gone back alone, and he would have nothing more to do with her? He hadn't spoken to her since, hadn't even looked at her. Maybe he would make friends with those other boys and she'd be on her own after all. She was still angry about Pittsburgh, too, but more afraid than angry. She should've just found her own way back and didn't know why she'd let Lenora stop her. It was as though her feet, turning around and following Lenora, had done her thinking for her. Maybe Eddie didn't care one way or the other. She was afraid she'd just been someone to ride with, and now he had new friends. She glanced up at Lenora, sitting on a rock at her side.

"I ought to save the corn silk for a dress," said Lenora. Elizabeth tried to smile, glad at least that she was eating.

"Ever seen blue corn?" asked one of the older men, who wore a wide straw hat.

No. Nobody ever had and they didn't believe there could be such a thing. But the man asking the question said he'd seen it himself near Albuquerque.

"And I've been to a corn dance, too. Now, the Indians, I'll tell you. *They* wouldn't let the government pay *them* not to harvest their crops. No siree."

Elizabeth listened as they talked on about corn bread and corn pones dripping with butter and honey, as the sparks soared above them like giant fireflies into a sky flushed with the rouge of twilight. The heat felt good on her face; the air was growing cooler by the minute.

"Couldn't you all shut up about food?" said one of Tony's friends, an older boy rolling a cigarette on his knee. "It's bad enough there's no butter or salt."

Lenora poked at a cob in the fire, rolling it over with a stick. Her fingers were long and dark and knobby, like the stick itself. Elizabeth looked down at Lenora's feet in dirty, white stockings and brown shoes tied shut with a piece of string laced through the top holes only. The middle of the shoes hung open.

"Had they heard about the big fire in Chicago?" The old man waved the smoke out of his face with his hat.

Elizabeth started. The cob of corn in her hand dropped to the ground between her feet. She couldn't ask "what fire?" herself.

"What fire?" said Eddie. He looked right at her, his eyes big and serious.

The man had been there all right. Had seen the red smoke billow up over the city like a circus tent. He seemed the oldest among them, had a gray, whiskery face.

Elizabeth stiffened. "I'm . . . I'm from Chicago," she blurted.

"Then you know all about it."

She shook her head and waited, afraid that he would tell her.

"I haven't been there in years," he said. "Full of Polacks." He laughed. "I don't mind the Polacks. They give good weddin' parties and make those nice little pastry dumplings. Half the city burned up."

"No," she said, her face still expressionless. "It couldn't

have." She looked at Eddie again, wishing he could stop the man from talking.

He rubbed his chin. "Oh, yes. Didn't you go to school? Didn't you learn about the fire in school? How that cow destroyed the whole city?" He sent a piece of the shack flying toward the center of the flames.

Her hands fell to her sides. Somebody snickered. "Oh," she said. "*That* fire." She reached down to pick up her corn and brushed off the dirt. Eddie was smiling, maybe thinking again she was just a foolish kid.

It was quiet. Nobody asked her why she'd left and she wished someone would, so she could hear herself say it out loud to someone new. That she had left home to help her family and would be back in no time at all.

"All this corn going to rot when people are starving. Now you tell *me.*" The older boy tossed a chewed-up cob over his shoulder. She thought his name was Albert.

"You don't *have* to starve in this country," said Eddie. "Look at us. There are ways."

"Huh," said Lenora.

Elizabeth saw the gazes, including Eddie's, come to rest on Lenora. He studied her now with narrow, cautious eyes.

But Lenora just smiled into the fire, yellow kernels protruding from the spaces between her teeth. "I don't mean to be rude, but I don't think because you've been hungry you know all there is to know about the subject in this whole country. If your train derails in the middle of Harlem, see then, you're in a bit more trouble. No corn growing wild, and the garbage cans are picked clean." She sucked at the kernels in her teeth with her tongue.

Elizabeth remembered something she'd often heard—that the colored "didn't know their place."

Eddie picked up another board and heaved it into the coals,

where it landed only a yard from the hem of Lenora's skirt. Elizabeth jumped. Sparks shot up twenty feet. Elizabeth waved the smoke from her eyes. Didn't Lenora know she was the only Negro here?

"If they're not going to harvest the crop, they ought to at least put a distillery out here for corn whiskey." It was Albert again. There were several shouts of assent. He laughed, then stared into Elizabeth's eyes until she looked away.

The voices seemed to blend together into one, round and round the fire, back and forth, dying away as the sparks flew upward. Elizabeth ate another piece of corn and listened. The coals were glowing like fat, red stars in the twilight. Thin shadows began to flicker across their faces as the fire died down.

"The coal car!" somebody shouted.

She followed the others as they walked ahead along the track a ways to the derailed coal car, where no train crew members hovered about. It wasn't stealing; everyone agreed. The coal would lie there on the ground and go to waste. They carried the smaller chunks back to the fire in armfuls. Soon the fire blazed and snapped again, its jagged edges reaching high.

Elizabeth dug the coal dust out from under her nails. The heat from the fire was making her sleepy—sleepy and thirsty. She saw a tall, sweaty glass of milk sitting on the kitchen table back home. "Can I have some more water?" Lenora reached behind her and pulled the jug from her bundle.

"You sure can," she said. " 'Those who thirst, come unto me.' You're so quiet, I almost forgot you were there."

Elizabeth tilted her head back and let the water run down her throat. She had to stop herself from drinking it all.

"You want some?" Lenora held the jug out to Eddie, perched on a log nearby.

He eyed the jug in her hand. "Naah."

"'Naah,'" Lenora repeated. "'Naah.' Why not? It ain't poison. It ain't contaminated. We don't have special water, you know."

"I didn't say so," he answered.

"You don't like me."

Eddie shrugged, looking away.

"You think I butted in back there on the train, don't you?"

"Yeah," he said sullenly, narrowing his eyes again. "I think it was none of your business."

"Maybe not," she said carefully, resting the jug on her knee. "If it was just you, I wouldn't have said anything. But then I guess you wouldn't 'a been talkin' out loud, unless it was to yourself. Then I would've kept my mouth shut for sure. I wasn't sure what you were up to, though, with that girl. Promising like that about manufacturing in Pittsburgh. Whoaaa . . ."

Eddie chewed on his lower lip and drew a circle in the dirt at his feet with a stick.

"I think I was right about Pittsburgh," said Lenora, pushing a clump of black hair back under her scarf. "It being dried up like Cleveland."

"Maybe," said Eddie, drawing a line through the middle of the circle.

"Isn't that why these other folks didn't get off there?"

"Okay," he blurted, "so maybe there's no work in Pittsburgh, either. I didn't lie about that tip I got." He was talking to Elizabeth now, the tone of his voice and the look in his eyes apologizing for what hadn't happened.

She thought if it was a dream, a nightmare, that she ought to wake up at just that moment. She opened her mouth but couldn't say anything.

"We're on a bad streak," he was saying. "It happens. If you want to go back, I'll see you get on the right train."

"Yeah, we'll help you," said Lenora. "Unless you want to go work in those fields just south. I don't know nothing about you . . ." She leaned forward, her eyes intent, the skirt draped wide between her knees. ". . . but if you're feeding yourself, at least you ain't taking up space at somebody else's table. An' you can always go back. I just hate to see you go off alone."

Elizabeth drew her arms in closer, suddenly cold and tired. "I don't know," she said. "I'll think about it in the morning." They were both looking at her, but she couldn't think of what else to say.

An old fellow came by passing out newspaper. She said "no thanks," but Eddie said to put it under her to cut out the dampness, so she did, and then she lay down with her sweater rolled up under her head. The sky was an inky blue-black, showered with stars. As she drifted off, Lenora and Eddie were still talking.

". . . I did stop her from going off alone, though, didn't I?"

"Where you from?"

"New York."

"That's why you said that about Harlem. . . ."

⇛ 14 ⇚

ELIZABETH WATCHED FROM A ROCK AS A CREW OF RAILROAD MEN feverishly operated their equipment, attempting to get the damaged cars out of the way and the rest of the train back in operation. It was morning, and she was hungry all over again. Her back was sore from sleeping on the bare, hard ground, and her face and hands were covered with mosquito bites. She still couldn't believe they were past Pittsburgh, out in the middle of nowhere, with nowhere really to go. Once a train passed them headed west, back to Pittsburgh and Cleveland, and maybe even Chicago. But she didn't make a move to get on it.

Eddie handed her a cup of hot, black coffee as he came to sit beside her on the broad, flat rock. "Those old men were nice enough to share," he said, glancing at her and looking off toward the train crew. "But Tony and Albert and those other kids are something, aren't they? Must be like running with a pack of wild dogs."

"I thought you probably liked them," she said, inhaling the aroma of the coffee, weak and watery as it was.

"Oh, they're all right." He brought the cup to his lips and blew. "They might be right about work in the fields, though, it being fall and harvest time for most crops. I guess you'll go back for sure now, won't you?"

"I suppose . . . I don't know." She sighed and turned her head toward the west.

"I thought you might hop that freighter going the other way. I really thought you'd take that one for sure, even though I was hoping. . . ."

"It seemed like it was going too fast," she said. She frowned, wondering if that were the truth, or if there were other reasons that kept her from going.

"Then I'm glad you didn't get on it. You always should remember the things I've told you, about being careful and all." Seeing her face, he said, "Mosquitoes were awful, weren't they?"

She took a longer look at him, saw his left eye was almost swollen shut, and smiled. "You look like you've been in a fight and lost it."

He laughed and nudged her with his shoulder. "They're buzzing around on full bellies—fuller than ours for sure."

"That corn roasting already still smells good, even after the five pieces I had last night."

"I know what you mean. Here comes Lenora. She seems all right, maybe not as goofy as I thought at first."

"Yeah?" Elizabeth replied, watching Lenora ease herself toward them and set herself down on the ground.

"I'm hungry," Lenora said, yawning, rubbing her eyes. "But I can't eat more corn, because what I put in me last night has all bloated up into one big solid kernel. It hurts."

"We were just talking about chasing down a chicken," said Eddie. "There's got to be a farm nearby."

"We were?" said Elizabeth. "Look who's goofy." She studied Lenora out of the corner of her eye, to see if Eddie was right. ". . . and then roasting it over a fire. I've done it plenty of times before. Add a few potatoes and, oh, man!"

"I never caught a chicken myself, but I saw some kids went after a pig once," said Lenora. "They chased it up to this river and thought they had it for sure, only the pig went in and swam away, and they didn't know how."

"Naah." Eddie pulled his knife from his pocket and picked up a stick. "I wouldn't want to chase down a pig."

"Why not?" asked Elizabeth, with only half her attention on the conversation. A wisp of cloud hung down around the horizon to the east. It was either that or a ribbon of steam from an approaching locomotive. She turned back to Eddie. "You know all about them, don't you? I'd think you'd be good at it."

"Well, I just got sick of pork is all," he said, shaving a thin curl of bark from the stick.

"You mean you'd pass some pork up now, if a pig waddled by?" Lenora looked over at Elizabeth with disbelief.

"No, it's just . . . it's different if you're around them all day. You get to know them, see?" He shrugged.

"You mean you get to be friends or what?" Lenora tilted her head to one side, eyeing him carefully.

"Well, not *friends* exactly. They're just like other pets, though. I had a favorite pig once, and I hid it in the closet when its turn came to be butchered." He stopped carving and stared down at the knife in his hand. "But my pa finally found it, and I couldn't eat pork for a *long* time after that. Oink," he said, wrinkling his nose. "Oink, oink."

Elizabeth smiled, then let herself laugh. She shook her head, then picked up a stone and threw it toward the tracks.

"Its name was Bob, because I'd had a best friend, Bob, who'd moved away, and I was lonely, so I named the pig Bob after him. I guess it's stupid of me to tell you this." He blushed.

"Bob," Lenora repeated, covering her mouth.

"Aww, be quiet. You'd be surprised about pigs. They're smarter and more human than you think!"

"More human than some folks, I'm sure," said Lenora, wiping her face with the end of her skirt. "I like animals, even the cat my sister drug home with a string hangin' along behind it everywhere it went, comin' out its heinie. . . ."

"Oh, no," said Elizabeth, gasping.

"Yeah. That's why she took it home, because she felt sorry for it. Must've eaten a ball of string or something."

"Sounds good to me about now," Eddie sighed, pushing the blade through a knot on the stick.

"My pa wouldn't let us bring home strays." Elizabeth was thinking back to the times she and Waldo had tried. Her pa wouldn't have it.

"Including me," said Eddie, laughing.

"Bob," Lenora repeated. "First, when I meet you, I think you're this tough guy and now you tell me about Bob. Maybe I don't know much about white boys."

Eddie pulled his cap down over his eyes.

"We did have a bird for a while," said Elizabeth, still thinking about home. "A canary. It used to sit on my mother's shoulder and drink from her coffee cup, and she let it."

Just then a bright red bird landed on a tree stump nearby, fluttering its wings, then dripping its head into a small hole full of water.

"Look," Eddie whispered. "A cardinal. I used to be for the Cardinals before I was for the Indians."

The bird flew off, startled by a sudden screeching of metal, as cranes began to drag a freight car off to the side of the tracks, spilling more coal out across the railroad bed. Coal. Elizabeth thought of how often she and Waldo had walked along the neighborhood tracks with the wagon, looking for coal to carry home for the winter, sometimes retrieving what a fireman in a passing train might toss to them. It was one way of helping out, just like Waldo needing help with his papers, and she'd never let him down. She thought about Waldo some more, and the money he'd hidden in his handlebars, and his scared face when Ivan had grabbed him by his collar. What Waldo needed was *not* to be scared, *not* to grow up as he was having to.

". . . I don't know the players much anymore," Eddie was saying. "I wonder if they still got that pitcher who won so many games in '31, the one with that dipsy-doodle in his curve ball. . . . Neither of you is listening."

"I'm sorry," said Lenora, pulling at her lower lip. "My mind just went off somewheres else. I was thinking about what you said before, about chicken and potatoes, and I was remembering all the ways you could cook a potato." And then she told them how she liked them best, just fried in butter. Elizabeth could see and smell the potatoes frying in butter; she could taste the butter and the potato and the salt and the pepper, each individually. And she thought that somebody who liked potatoes fried in butter couldn't be all that bad.

Lenora said she wondered if it was a potato farm the boys were heading off to.

Elizabeth slid a weed back and forth between her teeth, squinting at the reflection of the morning sun on the coal. The welts on her face were the size of nickels now, and she had to grit her teeth to keep from scratching them. After a while she and Lenora and Eddie got up, fetched a piece of corn each from the dying fire with sticks, and headed east down the track.

15

SOMETIMES ELIZABETH WOULD BE OUT IN THE FIELD, PICKING THE tobacco leaves or hauling a load of them to the drying shed, and she'd remember the oddest thing: Mrs. Bright asking her about the five food groups, for instance. Or the time Vera had a street shoe stolen out of her locker at school and had to wear her smelly gym shoes the rest of the day. The things she remembered seemed to bear no relation to her life now at all.

Gym shoes, and lockers, and going out with friends to the movies. She was storing those memories as you did winter clothes in the summer. She could pull one out and look at it if she wanted to, but there wasn't much point.

Remus Toland, a farmer, had hired all eight of them to work in his fields in western Virginia. He seemed to be a nice man, told them to take rest times out in the shade. But at first she still didn't think she could do it, stand there picking tobacco leaves for nearly ten hours a day in the sun. When she was sure she couldn't last another minute, Lenora would say, "Yes, you can do it. Just see if you can make it fifteen more minutes." Then fifteen minutes later, she'd say, "Try fifteen more." Then, "Look, you might as well finish the hour out." And somehow the hour would go by, and then another, and then there was a day gone, and then two. A few times Lenora was nice enough to bring her some water and once wrapped a wet cloth around her forehead.

Elizabeth had not been around colored folks before, did not know if Lenora would even eat the same kinds of food. She and Elizabeth slept at the far end of the bunkhouse, away from the boys, but they didn't spend much time talking. It seemed too hot to talk in the field, and in the evening they were too tired. But she'd stopped being afraid of Lenora, got used to her way of blurting things out, whatever was on her mind. Once while they were picking, she said, "I told you before, I thought Eddie was kinda wild. Well, he seems all right, so you can forget I said that, but I'd watch out for Albert if I was you. He's trash, he's got his eyes on you, and I wouldn't trust him."

It seemed Lenora was watching out for her, and that made her feel strange, to think a Negro person was looking after her like that. She didn't care for that Albert, though, how he always seemed to be watching her, and she tried not to be alone much, to stay near Lenora and Eddie.

She woke up once in the middle of the night to hear Lenora sniffling, and realized she was crying. Then Lenora began to talk very loud, right in her sleep. Elizabeth covered her ears, but she could still hear her. "JIM! JIM!" she called out.

She wondered who Jim was and asked her the next morning, even though she felt shy and figured it was none of her business. Lenora was surprised she'd called out for Jim. "I thought I got over him," she said from across the table, shaking her head.

Jim had been her husband, and he'd walked out after their daughter, Rebecca, had died of pneumonia. Lenora said instead of bringing them closer together, the death was like a wedge between them. "It's amazing what sorrow can do," she told Elizabeth. He couldn't take thinking it might have been his fault they couldn't pay a doctor. Elizabeth thought of her mother and Mrs. Vanhorn and then told Lenora she was sorry. It made her see Lenora in a different way, to think she'd been somebody's mother and wife.

The mattress springs squeaked as she rolled over onto her back. Overhead, the ceiling of the bunkhouse was strung with cobwebs.

It wasn't an easy life, but at the end of each day of hard work there was a hot meal waiting and after that a clean bed, a real mattress. That was more than she'd had in weeks, and she regretted admitting to herself that it wasn't enough. After a while she'd become used to the work, but she was restless, as if there were a clock in her head ticking off the minutes, the hours and days sliding by. She wanted more than food; she wanted money. And it wasn't going to fall from the sky.

Peering out the window, she could see Eddie ambling up the path toward the shed, barechested, mopping his forehead with his shirt. He *looked* like a farmer, as if he belonged here, and she remembered that her father had grown up on a farm in Sweden. Once he'd shown her a photograph of him standing in front of a cabin with his mother and sister, and they'd looked, to her, dirt poor. She'd never asked him anything about his life on the farm and now wished she had.

Eddie was closer now, and she leaned back away from the window so he wouldn't see her and think she'd been watching him. She wondered if Vera would think Eddie was cute. It was a silly thing to think about, really. Here he was, coming up the path with dirt and sweat running down his face and neck, his pants filthy and threadbare in places, and she was wondering if

Vera would think him "cute." *She* didn't think of him that way at all.

Sometimes she tried to picture what he was like before he'd left home, though it was hard to think of him being a regular guy, going to school and movies and dances, sitting around the table with his family. Being a kid growing up. It was a strain on her imagination to picture him in anything but overalls, but maybe he'd had nice clothes, even a suit and good shoes.

The spurts of anger toward him still came and went, and she remembered the first time she'd seen him, how he'd made finding work sound so easy. She supposed he was showing off then and hadn't meant to mislead her. If she had known it would be like this, would she have come? No, she didn't think so.

She wanted to talk to him now, see what he thought about moving on, looking for something better. Leaving a sure thing was risky, but she wanted money; she wanted it soon, and maybe "soon" was around the corner. Maybe the next town or just beyond? As Eddie said, it was a matter of timing.

She lifted her head from the mattress, hearing footsteps close by.

"Too hot to sleep, ain't it?"

It was Albert, his arms folded across a grayish-white under-shirt, whispering down at her. She did not like him, never had, and shrugged her shoulders to show she wasn't interested in talking. She hoped he could not read the worry in her face, as she knew he was not supposed to cross over to their side of the bunkhouse.

"Me, neither," he said. "Got a game of craps going back there. Want to watch?"

She shook her head. The lower half of his face was covered with a dark shadow. He didn't often bother to shave.

He sighed loudly, for effect. "Why not? Eddie's not around." He grinned, a small, thin scar trembling under his eyes, and swatted a fly buzzing around his face. "No harm in watching. Aren't you lonely back here, anyway? Don't you want some company. . . ? A girl shouldn't be by herself so much. . . ."

She had raised herself up onto her elbows just as Eddie came through the screen door and started for the boys' end of the bunkhouse. Seeing Albert by Elizabeth's bed, he came to a dead halt, dug his hands into his pockets, and began to stroll toward them.

"Hey, Albert," he said evenly, cocking his head to one side. "Whacha doing back here?"

"Keeping her company," said Albert, his smile quivering a bit at the corners of his mouth.

Eddie hitched up his pants. "Well, that's nice of you, Albert. I know what a thoughtful person you are, but I thought we didn't come over to the girls' side, Albert. How come everybody knows that but you?"

"Well, maybe nobody *wanted* to but me. Myself, I can't figure why Lenora's down at this end and not you. What's wrong with you, Eddie? Afraid of girls or something?" He leered, standing with his feet spread wide apart.

Elizabeth sat up, swallowing hard. "It's all right, Eddie," she blurted. "Just go on back there, both of you, where you're supposed to be."

"I never have liked you," said Eddie. "Not from the first time I saw you. . . ." Then he had Albert by the collar, shoving him up against the wall.

Lenora jumped in her sleep and sat up in the next bed. "What? What?" she hollered.

"Stop it!" Elizabeth shouted. But they were already rolling around on the floor, one of them popping the other with his fist, then the other swinging back. Elizabeth got up off her bed and ran out the door.

⇾≫ 16 ≪⇽

SHE HAD TOO MUCH TIME TO THINK NOW, THE TRIP TO ATLANTA
on a Southern Railway freight car seeming endless. It had taken
her, Lenora, and Eddie out of Virginia by way of Lynchburg and
Roanoke, then through the Blue Ridge Mountains and Charlotte,
North Carolina, down across the upper left-hand corner of South
Carolina and on into the red clay hills of Georgia. She'd monitored
their route on the map, wishing they'd passed through the Chattahoochee National Forest just because of the sound of the name.

The open map lay on the rough-hewn floor beside her. "Atlanta," she read again. She shifted her weight onto the opposite
knee and brushed the dirt off the front of an old pair of trousers
given to her by Sarah, the farmer's wife. All she knew about
Atlanta was what she'd learned in school—the Civil War and the
Confederacy. She didn't know much else, except for the rumors
about its being so hard on vagrants.

"King of hearts takes it, Eddie. Your shuffle." Lenora threw her cards down and yawned. "Sure you don't want in on this hand, Elizabeth?"

"No, thanks. We're almost to Atlanta." She didn't like cards that much, anyway. They'd always bored her, seeming like something that old people did as a way of passing the time. It still seemed that way, even though she'd given up and played a few hands because there was nothing else to do.

Sometimes she studied the map, reading aloud the names of towns that struck her as odd or funny or interesting. Miller's Tavern, Woolwine, Burning Springs, Hazard, and Point of Rocks, in Virginia. Pilot Mountain, Pumpkin Town, Bat Cave, Thermal City, Turtletown and Ducktown, Norway, Gardners Store, Tuxedo, and Cashiers, in the Carolinas. If they had gone through the Chattahoochee National Forest, they could have stopped at Loving, at Roy, Helen, Naomi, or Margret, and she would remember to tell Vera that she'd almost gone to Hollywood. Which made her think of the Hollywood Grill on Michigan Avenue, where she and Vera used to go for colas and hamburgers on Saturday afternoons when they'd had the money. She forced herself not to think about it now.

"Tallapoosa, Chickamauga, Tuckasegee, Ahoskie," she read out loud.

"What in hell . . ." said Eddie, scowling at his cards. He scratched at his bare chest, the suspenders hanging free down the front of his pants.

"Ahoskie," she continued. "I guess that could be Indian or Polish. Then here's Warsaw. That's Polish for sure. And Scotland *Neck.* Why would you name a town 'Scotland Neck'?" He and Lenora didn't seem to be listening. "Athens, Sparta, Macedonia, Dublin, and Vienna, all here in Georgia." She sneezed, reaching into her pocket for a rag.

"Chattahoochee, God bless you," said Lenora. "Why go

around the world when you can just go to Georgia? Pair 'a queens, Eddie. Ha, ha." She winked at Elizabeth. "My stomach is growling, mad because I've stopped feeding it again."

This time, it was she who'd had to talk Lenora into coming. Lenora didn't want to go south, said if she couldn't get regular work in the north, she surely wouldn't get it in the south. But she'd finally agreed, saying she'd go because she liked them both, and if they both got hired in that storage place Tony told them about and she didn't, well, she could turn around and go back if she wanted to.

But all the way from the farm in Virginia down into Georgia, Elizabeth worried if it was the right thing to do. Being back on the road again made her fearful and anxious, a persistent gnawing inside her stomach. Once the bread was gone, what would they eat, and where would they get it? What would they do, once they got to Atlanta? Too much time in which to think.

". . . so we have to make a rule," Eddie was saying, sitting cross-legged nearby. "Not to talk about food if we don't have any, unless it's ideas about getting some, all right? I used to ride with this guy who blabbered all the time about his mother's cooking and all his favorite foods. Custard pie, custard pie, *custard pie!* If I'd 'a had one, I would've thrown it in his face." He leaned forward to see the card Lenora threw down. "Nuts." He searched the cards in his hand, then scratched his head under his cap. "But we'll get this job, anyway, cause Tony's brother is there, and we got an 'in.' Just the same, it's a good rule to keep. How you doing there, Elizabeth? Keeping yourself amused?"

She nodded, still poring over the map, trying to figure the miles from Chicago to Atlanta.

"Okay, here we go. Two on, two out, bottom of the ninth. Indians down by one. Frey steps to the plate. . . ." He flung a card on top of Lenora's. "He swings! King of hearts! Going, going, gone! IT'S OVER THE LEFT FIELD FENCE!" He threw up his arms and let out a cheer.

"No, it ain't," said Lenora. She tossed down an ace, face up. "Ace of diamonds. Game's over, I win."

Eddie groaned, dropping his head onto his knees. "Robbed! A leaping catch by Gehrig wins the game."

"It wasn't the Yankees."

"Doesn't matter," he mumbled.

"It was the Kings."

"The Kings?" he said, lifting his head. "Who're *they?*"

"A Negro team, but it doesn't matter, because you cheated. You pulled that card out of your hat. I saw." She shook a bony finger in his face.

"Did not!" He lifted his hat to show her, smiling broadly.

Sometimes Elizabeth tried to see Lenora and Eddie through her parents' eyes. Maybe her father would feel bad for Lenora, even though she was Negro. Maybe he would see the holes in her clothes, the skin sagging all over, even over the little bones under her eyes, and say, "The poor woman. It isn't right." Just as he would say about anyone, even his own wife.

She could hear him above the noise of the train clipping along. "Roosevelt hasn't done much for the poor working stiff. The New Deal is a rotten deal, *ja.*"

And her ma. Would what *she* think? It didn't matter what she thought. She would give Lenora food from her own garden, if there had been any left. If she thought something bad, she would keep it to herself.

What would they think of Eddie? She looked at him, his trousers hanging low over his hips, his dark hair growing thick down the back of his neck, and decided not to dwell on it. "Tramp needs a haircut," she heard her pa say. It was hard to think that they were going on with their lives without her, but she supposed

119

they were. She *wanted* them to, after all, she argued silently.
Eddie had his knife out, slicing away the green part on the
last hunk of bread.

The dust swirled up around them in a thin, red cloud like
a swarm of mosquitoes. Still, Elizabeth could not miss the first
billboard that greeted them as they approached the city the last
mile or so on foot, on an unpaved road.

VAGRANTS BEWARE!
STIFF JAIL SENTENCES
OR CHAIN GANG DUTY.
NO FIRST-TIME LENIENCY.

"I've heard of it happening," said Eddie. "The chain gang
for just passing through! Good thing we got that address from
Tony."

A few hundred yards down the road they came to a second
billboard. It said:

I AM THE WAY, THE TRUTH AND THE LIFE.
NO MAN COMETH UNTO THE FATHER EXCEPT
BY ME.
JOHN 14:6

Elizabeth remembered that she had a bookmark back home
with that verse written on it. And, when she was younger, a small
magic, white cross above her bed that said: "Ye are the light of
the world." At night she'd set it beneath a lamp before she went
to bed and then it would glow in the dark until she fell asleep.
But that was in another lifetime. . . .

They slipped underneath a tarp in the back of a pickup while the truck was parked beside a gas pump and rode the rest of the way into the city on a mountain of peaches. Every so often, Elizabeth would feel a peach give way, its juice seeping into her shirt or the seat of her pants. When the truck came to a stop and cut its engine, she grabbed a few of the smashed peaches, slid out the back, and ran.

The truck had stopped in the center of a "farmer's market," rows of fresh produce stands, huge and sometimes unattended barrels of peaches, bananas, plums and melons, potatoes and tomatoes. She tried not to look at the mounds of fruits and vegetables as she, Eddie, and Lenora made their way down the aisles, and was relieved when the last barrel was behind them.

They kept on walking, past houses that were big, with fancy iron balconies, but run-down and in need of fresh paint. Their windows opened out onto the noisy street, which bustled with shoppers, fruit and peanut vendors with pushcarts, scissors grinders and knife sharpeners outshouting each other for business. Elizabeth had never seen anything like it.

They stopped an old couple on the street for directions to the address they had. "Keep going," said the woman, looking at the three of them quizzically. "You're almost there. Other side of Decatur." She turned to the man beside her and shook her head.

"I still don't know what a job in storage could be," said Elizabeth, lumbering along between Lenora and Eddie. "Maybe a cannery, you think? Or some kind of new refrigeration?" She'd seen her mother do a lot of canning other summers and had helped her fill and seal the jars now and then.

"I don't know," said Lenora. "But I don't think they'll hire me."

They were tired and hungry again by the time they got to Decatur Street, which was full of more colored folks than Elizabeth had ever seen. Broken-down furniture and bits of junk littered the sidewalk in front of stores and pawn shops; old clothes were strung between buildings. She heard the slapping of billiard balls and curses and laughter from inside dark, smoky places, and she wanted to hurry past them.

"I'm so hungry I could eat one of 'em raw," sighed Lenora, as they passed a shriveled-looking old colored man hovering over a big tub of water. "FISH! FISH!" he sang, his lips peeled back over smooth, pink gums.

The shops gave way to shacks, set against each other like rows of dominoes. Elizabeth stopped hurrying. She was no longer afraid, staring at the half-dressed colored kids swarming the porches, women hanging laundry and chasing after babies crawling in the dirt. There were colored parts of Chicago you could see from the train to downtown. But she'd never *walked* among them, did not know it would feel like being in another country. It all made her feel strange, as if she ought to say something to Lenora, that she was sorry or something. But that didn't seem right, either. Sorry for what? That Lenora was colored? That the colored here seemed poorer than she'd imagined people could be?

"Stop whistling," she murmured to Eddie on her right.

"Why?"

"I don't know. It just doesn't seem right."

⇢≫ 17 ≪⇠

"THERE'S A MISTAKE HERE SOMEWHERE," ELIZABETH MURMURED, squinting at the scrawl of letters and numbers on the scrap of paper in her hand. She glanced back up at the sign towering above them, which read PEACEFUL VALLEY in green letters tastefully outlined in black.

"It's a *cemetery.*" Eddie gaped at the sign with his hands on his hips.

"Lord, it is," said Lenora, sighing and lowering herself to the curb. "We're whipped but good. We might as well sign up now."

"A cemetery." Elizabeth dropped her hands to her side, turning to Eddie. "You suppose it could be work in groundskeeping or something?"

"Don't you get it?" he muttered. "It's supposed to be a joke. Storage—a cemetery. Don't you get it? Some joke all right."

She turned her gaze back to Peaceful Valley, her eyes sweeping over the spacious lawns studded with gray stone and marble fixtures. She could not believe it, but there it was. A *cemetery*. She felt her eyes well with tears and wiped a grimy hand across her forehead. "It's so mean."

"It was Albert put Tony up to it. I'll bet ya." The veins in Eddie's neck stood out; his fist beat against the side of his leg. "If I ever lay eyes on that bastard. . . ."

"Won't do us any good now, will it?" Lenora lifted her head, her face creased with worry and fatigue. "Now what? We can't just go beggin' on the streets in Atlanta. Not me, especially. Lord, have mercy. It never ends, does it?"

Elizabeth slumped to the curb beside her, head in her hands.

"Tony said his brother was fixed for good," said Eddie, still standing. "Said he didn't have to do no more looking." He dropped to the street with a hard, bitter laugh.

"Oh, shush." Lenora reached to swat him on the shoulder. "Stop it, Eddie. We have to think. This is Atlanta, remember?"

"What a jerk . . . they're back there laughing at us right now! Well, who knows, maybe I ought to check at the office anyway. Maybe what with the way things are, business is booming." He looked at Elizabeth and shrugged.

"Maybe those people in there are better off." Elizabeth nodded toward the cemetery, pressing her lips together until they hurt.

"Oh, c'mon." Eddie nudged her with his elbow. "Once I worked the *graveyard* shift, chopping pickles for White Castle. I ate so many hamburgers and milkshakes this one night, the manager comes back to me and says, 'You still hungry, Eddie?' And I says, 'Yeah,' real smart-alecky, even though I wasn't. He says, 'Good,' then takes me by the collar and shoves my head into this big vat of pickles. Ain't had a pickle since." He stood up, chuckling, and took Lenora and Elizabeth each by the hand. "Let's go. We'll think of something."

But Elizabeth knew, as they headed back toward the center of town, that neither he nor Lenora had any more idea than she about where to go next. Her calves hurt from walking. Her feet burned where the soles had worn through. She felt in her pocket for the fifty cents Remus Toland had sent them each off with. She'd be willing to spend it all on something to eat and drink.

On Ponce de Leon they turned right, stopping in front of a sign in the window of a drugstore. It said:

30¢ FOUNTAIN LUNCH SPECIAL
Baked Spiced Ham with Raisin Sauce
Corn Sticks, Cole Slaw, Choice of Two
Vegetables, and Choice of Tea, Coffee,
Buttermilk or Root Beer.

"Oh," Elizabeth sighed, her face pressed to the glass. There were people eating at the counter, and she could already taste the ham in the raisin sauce. "Let's just eat here, all right?"

But Eddie and Lenora were looking at another sign taped to the door. It said NO COLORED.

She got a glimpse of Lenora's face, her wounded surprise, before she turned and stomped off. Elizabeth wanted to tear after her right then, afraid she would lose Lenora in the crowd, but Eddie held her back. They trailed along behind instead, weaving in and out of the crowd, running through red lights to keep her in sight. They caught up with her between Eighth and Ninth streets.

Lenora's eyes blazed, as if she had a fire inside her. Racing along beside her, Elizabeth was sure she could feel the heat.

They crept inside a toolshed out back of a small house just after dusk, a big red-orange moon hanging overhead like a smooth Georgia peach. Because the shed smelled of kerosene or paint thinner, they propped the door open with a brick and covered the dirt floor with a white chenille bedspread spotted with paint. They'd found it on a countertop. Elizabeth removed her shoes, which were lined with cardboard to save what was left of the soles, and fell onto the bedspread. Her head ached and her stomach hurt, as though it had caved in on itself. She knew she was a selfish person for sure, but she couldn't help thinking if Lenora hadn't been colored they would have eaten by now. Lenora lay down beside her, and she turned her face away, afraid the selfishness would be plain to see.

"I can't sleep with you standing," Lenora said to Eddie. He leaned against a workbench, fingering the handle of a shovel. "Besides, with the moon out someone could see you." Her voice sounded different now, flat, without feeling.

"Yeah, I guess," said Eddie. He heaved a sigh like an old man and sat down on the bedspread.

Elizabeth rested her head in the crook of her arm. She closed her eyes, wanting to fall asleep right away, but they wouldn't stay shut. There were moon shadows all across the ceiling.

". . . my own fault," Lenora was saying. "I heard about stuff like that and shouldn't have come. Maybe I wanted to see it with my own eyes, and now I have."

"The hell it's your fault," said Eddie. "I should've gone in and flattened the guy with one punch." He lay back and lowered his hat over his eyes.

"They'd 'a called you a Commie and threw you in the slammer," said Lenora. "God, I'm so *tired,* all of a sudden. I'd like to lie here for days just like this. I wish we hadn't left the farm. *They* didn't seem to care I was colored, treated me like anyone else."

The shadows overhead fluttered as the leaves of a tree shivered, rustling against the window.

Elizabeth turned her head toward Lenora. She thought

maybe her cheek was wet. "It's the worst thing I've ever seen," she whispered. "I mean it, Lenora. Let's get out of Atlanta tomorrow." She lifted herself onto her elbows. "I don't want to stay here, either." She wanted to put her arms around Lenora but felt shy and afraid.

"Fine," said Eddie, "but where'll we go? Guess I'm running out of ideas. I thought that job was a sure thing and look what happened. I don't want to go back north, neither, not for the winter." He took off a shoe and flung it across the shed. "I still wish I would've punched the lights out of that soda jerk."

Elizabeth swallowed as the dark deepened around them. Cooler air seeped in through the cracks, gently stirring the hair on her arms. She could see the stars coming out through a little window above them.

"The thing is," Lenora went on. "It's my country, too. Just as much as those people eating inside, it's *my country, too!*" Her voice quivered and finally broke.

"I should've . . ." Eddie began.

"Okay," said Lenora. "Okay."

Elizabeth brushed her hand across Lenora's. "Oh, Lenora," she said. "I'm sorry." Then she lay back down and shut her eyes again. The inside of her mouth and her throat felt like cotton. Worse maybe. Rough and blistery, like the bottom of her feet. She closed her eyes and saw a tall, sweaty glass of root beer on the gray marble counter in the drugstore. She brought the straw to her mouth and sipped. The cold liquid swirled about her mouth and ran down her throat.

She awoke to the sound of footsteps on the pavement outside, gradually receding into the distance. She thought she'd been thirsty at night, but now she figured she knew what the word meant.

She'd covered herself during the night with her jacket and carefully laid it aside now, maneuvering herself out from between Eddie and Lenora and slipping through the toolshed door. A large swing took up half the back porch of the house out front. It could have been anybody's house anywhere, her own, even. The blinds on the back windows were drawn so she could not see inside. She took a step forward on the grass, the dew soaking her bare feet, and then another, until she'd reached the bottom step. Next to the swing, on the doormat, stood a bottle of fresh milk, glistening at her in the pale morning light like an unguarded golden treasure, a gem. She went up the back stairs until she was standing beside it, looking down. She leaned over. . . .

The back door opened. She saw the man's face and for a moment she was surprised that she did not know him. He stuck his arm out, grabbed her roughly by the shoulder and drew her inside.

"Helen!" the man yelled. "Look what I found on the porch!"

Elizabeth saw a woman in the kitchen, wringing her hands. The woman raised her hand to cover her mouth, as her own mother would have done.

"Oh, Hank, she's only a child."

"Sure she is. Tell her what I caught you at." He still had ahold of Elizabeth's shoulder and shook it.

"Hank! Let her go!"

"TELL HER WHAT I CAUGHT YOU AT!"

Elizabeth looked at him blankly, unable to speak.

"Well, of course she won't say. She can tell the cops. *They'll* get it out of her."

"Oh, Hank, let go of her!"

"The HELL I will!"

He gripped her wrist harder, reaching for the phone. Elizabeth saw him dial, heard him speak into the mouthpiece, and drop it back into the receiver on the wall, as though she were watching a scene from a movie.

"There. They said five minutes. Hoodlums don't wait to become hoodlums until they're twenty-one, you know. I'm doing her a favor. Think of it that way, Helen."

"Maybe she's *hungry*, Hank."

"So? Am I my brother's keeper? Is it up to me to feed the masses?"

"Maybe." Hank's wife stepped out the back door, brought in the bottle of milk, and set it on the table.

Elizabeth watched the woman undo the cap and pour some into a cup, then hand it to her. She took the cup and drank. "Thank you," she said, and set the cup back on the table.

"Where're you from?" asked the man's wife.

"Chicago."

"She's from Chicago, Hank. A regular city like ours. Call them back and tell them not to come."

"Chicago. It figures," said Hank. He left the room to answer the door.

It *was* only a movie, Elizabeth thought. The two cops strolling into the kitchen, the handcuffs dangling from their belts. She answered their questions but later couldn't remember what they'd asked. She found herself in the back of a squad car. But it was not her, really. She was back in the State Theater, watching it happen to someone else on the movie screen in front of her. Maybe it was Garbo or Dietrich or Hepburn, and any minute they would know what to do to keep from going to jail. . . .

129

⇥⇥ 18 ⇤⇤

THE OFFICER ON THE PASSENGER SIDE HEAVED A SIGH AND ROLLED down his window as they pulled into traffic, letting a warm, fragrant breeze replace the smell of tobacco smoke and leather inside the car. From the backseat, Elizabeth looked out at the streets of Atlanta coming to life. The squad car swerved to avoid a bicyclist as it turned a corner. When it came to a stop at a red light, the children in the next car mashed their faces against the windows to get a better look.

They seemed to be heading downtown. After a while, they pulled up in front of a large, square, red brick building.

"Well, here's the hotel," said the officer behind the wheel. "Meals provided, but the shower's a ways down the hall." He laughed at his joke, then turned and looked at Elizabeth. "Stop worrying," he said. "They're not going to throw away the key."

She was surprised when they led her into a big office, in which men and women clacked away at typewriters and talked on the telephone. She sat in a straight-backed wooden chair beside a desk while a man in a white shirt rolled up to his elbows filled out some forms. He asked three times for the names and address of her parents and three times she remembered why she'd left and said nothing.

Threads of red and green ran through the gray tile floor. She gave him her height and weight and birthday and tried to look at the tile instead of into the man's probing dark eyes. He asked her if she thought stealing was a serious thing and she said yes. He asked if she thought she would likely do it again, and she thought about trying to explain but gave him a simple no. Did her parents go to church? Yes, they did, but not every Sunday. Did she go to church herself? Yes, her parents sent her and Waldo to Sunday school. She could see the huge stone building, stern, imposing, and gray like Rev. Olafsson himself.

She wanted to tell the man behind the desk that she'd been interviewed before, only it had been for work, but she was afraid to say anything. She sat with her fingers intertwined on her knees.

He said it was a lucky thing she'd been caught early on, and he did not believe her when she said she was going to get a job and send money home. He leaned back in his swivel chair and laughed.

A short, uniformed woman came to get her, unlocking a thick, green door with a huge ring of keys. "You smell like turpentine," she said, wrinkling her nose. "And *peaches*. What've you been up to?"

Elizabeth did not mind the shower. The water was hot and soapy as it would've been at home. Yes, she went to church. Cleansed by the Blood of the Lamb, she heard herself think, as the drain beneath her feet slurped up the dirty water.

They gave her shoes, because she'd left her own in the shed, and a navy blue smock. She dropped it over her head and followed

131

the matron down a hallway to a large room, blue with hundreds—at first she thought thousands—of smocked women seated at oblong tables. Lunch was a liquidy bean thing and sour, stale bread, as in a soup kitchen, only she supposed you couldn't get up and leave when you were done. She ate it, keeping her head down. Maybe she *was* only in a soup kitchen, a mission, like the ones back in Cleveland and other towns they'd been in.

They put her in a cell with two women, one stout and gray, the other younger and frailer looking, and a pregnant girl with a round, pink face. Her ears hurt when the door clanged shut behind her.

"Hi, I'm Thelma. Welcome to Happy House." The portly woman thrust forward her hand and Elizabeth shook it.

"Top bunk is yours, Elizabeth. They told me your name. It's a pretty one. I'm sorry you're here but I'm glad you're in with us. You've never been in jail before, I can tell just by looking that you've been living on the street, right, and they got you for just some little thing, like passing through or waiting for handouts."

Elizabeth nodded, looking down at the floor. She saw the bottle again on the doormat, as pure and white as a new snowfall. A thief *and* a liar.

"Too bad," said Thelma, lifting up and down on her stockinged toes. "They think the air ain't free to breathe in this city." She shook her graying head, which blended into the wall behind her. Elizabeth saw she could look in any direction, the walls, the floor, the ceiling and see only gray.

"It just isn't right, but don't worry, you'll get out when you give them an address back home. Any address will get you a free ticket back, if that's what you want. Elizabeth, this is Ginger. You can see how she spends her time."

"Oh, you damn busybody," said Ginger. She folded her arms

across her smock, which was stretched tight over her bulbous middle.

"And this is Mary. Mary, stop banging your head on the toilet and smile. She doesn't talk. They ought to send her to a hospital and not keep her here. This is City. No one stays here long, anyway. Like me. I'm on my way to the pen. They think I'm a troublemaker. Want to play checkers?"

Thelma had to remind Elizabeth over and over when it was her turn to move. The pregnant girl, Ginger, never stopped talking. She prattled on and on about how she was going to do a better job on her boyfriend the next time, maybe use an iron skillet instead of a flower pot.

"She's a Yankee," Ginger said once to Thelma, as if Elizabeth weren't there. As how her pa sometimes would talk about her mother.

"Nothing wrong in that," drawled Thelma. "They just eat funny food. Your move, Elizabeth."

"And they take to the colored race, too."

Elizabeth looked up from the game. How had she known about Lenora? Ginger was filing her nails on the top bunk against the adjacent wall, elbows planted on the shelf of her stomach.

She would probably never see Eddie or Lenora again. The cops might've sent them running, and she didn't blame them. No, she wouldn't blame either of them for not waiting around, and she wouldn't know how to find them anyway. She bit her bottom lip and then bit down harder. She'd messed up but good.

"Do they?" asked Thelma. "Well, they're in good company. Abraham Lincoln liked them, too."

"I think you're a Communist, Thelma. Or a Yankee at heart. A real southern girl wouldn't go on like that."

"This is the twentieth century, Ginger. Things are going to

change and it's a mighty good thing." Thelma undid a pincurl and rewound it tighter, holding the bobby pin between her teeth. Then she picked up a checker and jumped one of Elizabeth's queens.

"Yeah, look at all them changes," said Ginger. "When've you ever seen so many people poor as dirt? If the streets could only talk. . . ."

"That's right, Gin, if the streets could talk. If the streets could talk, we'd hear the little children ask their mommies why some people in this country get to eat and others don't. . . ."

"Okay, all right," said Ginger. "If Shaeffer had been working instead of moping about the house and bothering me, I wouldn't be here. And I wouldn't be this *way*, either."

"Well, I hope you can feed it," said Thelma. "What do *you* think, Mary?"

The mute lady was engrossed in picking a hangnail. She went on with it as if she hadn't heard a word.

"I still say," said Ginger, "you're red as half that checker board."

"She refuses to play with me, Elizabeth, because she doesn't like either color, you see. So I'm glad you're here, even if your mind's not on the game. Yoo-hoo, anybody home in there?"

Elizabeth looked up from the board. She knew how to play well. Her pa had taught her when she was small and she remembered the first time she'd beat him and spilled hot cocoa on the rug in her excitement. Hot cocoa made with milk and a creamy white marshmallow floating in the center.

She had to use the toilet but it sat naked at the end of the cell.

"Aren't we a foursome?" said Thelma. "You and Ginger and me and Mary. We should be off to a mother-daughter tea instead of in jail."

"You can be *their* mother, not mine." Ginger rolled her eyes toward the ceiling.

"She's like a queen bee, that Ginger." Thelma pulled a cigarette from her pocket and slipped it into her mouth. "She just sits there all day filing those nails. She's got to be down to the bone by now."

Mary began to hum underneath her blanket.

"Oh, yeah," said Thelma. "She doesn't talk, but she sings herself to sleep. If we all pretend to take naps, she'll stop singing sooner." She slid the checkerboard under her mattress. Elizabeth pulled herself up to the top bunk and lay down.

> *Left my gal in the mountains,*
> *Left her standin' in the rain,*
> *Went down to the railroad,*
> *Caught myself a midnight train,*
> *Beat my way to Georgia. . . .*

Mary's voice was small, nasal and twangy, like someone plucking a single string of a guitar. Elizabeth drifted, neither asleep nor awake, until the cell door was opened for dinner.

She realized later that night that whatever it was they'd had for dinner didn't agree with her. In bed she felt as though she were back in a swaying boxcar, though nothing but Thelma was moving beneath her. Thelma rolled over, the bed shimmied, and Elizabeth's hand gripped the frame of the bed. Mary was not yet asleep.

> *They put the handcuffs on me,*
> *Put me on a Pullman train,*
> *Took me to Atlanta,*
> *And tied me with a ball and chain.*

Left my gal in the mountains,
Left her waiting all alone. . . .

She lost her whole dinner and more it seemed, and when she was too weak to make it up to the top bunk, Thelma traded hers. Then Thelma's hand was at the back of her head, holding it up over the toilet bowl.

"There, there, let's wipe away those tears while we're at it."

"I can't stand it no more," said Ginger. "I'm going to start puking myself and then I could throw up the baby."

Thelma said she couldn't throw up a baby because it wasn't in her stomach and the girl pointed to her stomach and said, "What do you call this if it ain't my belly?" Thelma laughed and said it was her womb, and she would know the difference sure enough when the baby wanted out.

The prison bars all around me,
A guard walkin' by the door.
My heart is sad and lonely,
'Cause I'll never see my gal no more.

Elizabeth covered her ears, and tried to shut from her mind what Ginger said about her baby. For some reason it made her sicker. During the night another matron took her upstairs and locked her up alone in something that seemed half like a cell and half like a regular room, because it had a wooden door with bars only in the window. They couldn't take chances, the woman said, what with her fever and all the typhoid and diphtheria going around. Elizabeth did not mind the quiet and the bed not moving beneath her. Up above her was a small, square window through which she could see a round belly of a moon against a pitch-black sky. It was the same moon as the night before, but slit cleanly down the middle by a silver bar, just like the past and the future.

She didn't wake up until it was light, when the door slamming shut startled her awake. The matron was back to take her temperature and encouraged her to try some hot cereal and tea. She managed the tea but couldn't even look at the cereal and fell back asleep until late afternoon, when she was roused awake again and told to get into her street clothes.

Why hadn't she told them she had a brother in Atlanta? They would have called him right away!

She stumbled sleepily to the front desk.

"If we ever catch you on the street again, you will dearly regret it, brother or not," said the officer behind the counter.

Her "brother" wore a navy blue suit and hat, and he lowered his head and shook it when Elizabeth approached, as if he were ashamed to know her. Then he removed his glasses and wiped his eyes. She thought, at first, that it was Rev. Olafsson.

He shook the matron's hand and then took Elizabeth by her arm and led her out the front door. "Don't say a word. Just follow me," he cautioned out of the side of his mouth.

She knew by then it was Eddie and did as he said, shielding her eyes from the glare of the late afternoon sun on the steps. The sidewalk was full of pedestrians, and she would have liked to disappear among them, she was so ashamed. And yet, because she was also so happy and relieved to see him, she turned and put a trembling hand on his arm.

"Oh, Eddie . . . " she began. She looked up into his thin face, his dark, serious eyes under the wide blue brim. "I've been in jail."

"Well, I know," he said. "Let's not talk here, though. Let's get away from this place." He took hold of her arm again, guiding her down to the sidewalk and along the street as if she wouldn't be able to make it on her own.

"Elizabeth," he said, sighing and lowering himself to the

curb. "Are you okay? You look all right, except you're so pale." He pulled her down to the curb beside him.

"I . . . I guess I'm all right." She covered her face with her hands, trying to hold back the tears.

He picked at a hangnail on his thumb, then suddenly looked up and slipped his arm around her shoulder. "Look, it's okay to go ahead and cry and everything."

She shook her head and bit her lip.

"When you feel like it, tell me what happened. But you don't have to yet. We can sit here for a while and not talk, or we can start walking back to the yard. Whatever you want. You just say it, all right?"

She nodded, the tears slipping through her fingers. He was the nicest boy she'd ever met. It made the tears come faster, and she hurried to brush them away. "It was in the morning," she tried to begin. "The milk was just sitting out there and I was so thirsty. . . ." Her voice broke and she lowered her head, still dizzy from the fever.

"Yeah," he said, tossing his hat to the ground. "I woke up once and you were there, and the next time you weren't. I couldn't figure it out. So I got up and went outside and then this guy comes running out of that front porch like a crazy man. I thought he was going to shoot me. Said if I was a friend of yours I should 'git.' *Then* he sees Lenora. Brother! Grabs me by the shirt and shoves me. Tells me to take 'my nigger' with me."

Elizabeth cringed. She could see the man's face as if he were right in front of her, his arm reaching out for her, and the kitchen, too, in a thin, yellow light. She put her hand on her stomach, feeling the nausea again.

"So you were taking his milk?" he said, turning to look at her.

She shrugged. "I guess. I don't know, maybe I was trying to when he came out. I never actually touched it." She dried a lone tear quivering off the end of her chin.

"That's not so bad. Happens all the time. What're we supposed to do, starve?" He took off his jacket and laid it across his lap. "That man's the one should be in jail, turning you in. He's the kind who's so afraid what's happened to us could happen to him. You know? That's why he did it. It wasn't because of the milk. Look at you, poor thing. They said you were sick in there. Is that right?"

She nodded, suddenly wanting to lie down somewhere in the shade.

"It's from not eating right. You're all worn out. We've got to get regular food. I'm going to get us some tonight. I feel so bad, like it's all my fault. You're too nice, Elizabeth. This shouldn't have happened to you. It should've been me. I was the one made you promises and let you down. All these hunches and tips— Cleveland, Pittsburgh, Atlanta. I'm nothin', a loser. . . ." He picked up a stone and hurled it across the street.

She lifted her head and looked away from him, at the cars slowly passing by them down the boulevard. "It's nice of you to say that, but no, it's not your fault. I did it on my own. I left Chicago to go with you on my own. You didn't *make* me. It was my own idea. I can't blame you anymore when things don't go right."

"You got guts, Elizabeth. I ain't even been to jail."

"Where'd you get those clothes?" she asked, examining his outfit head to foot.

"Oh, it's the ol' pole-through-the-window trick. Stick a long pole through somebody's open window and lift out the clothes. They say 'clothes don't make the man,' but I sure feel different dressed like this. I've got to return them soon."

He'd had to steal to get her out of jail. It was as she'd learned in Sunday school, that one lie always led to another. "Where's Lenora?" she asked, as they got up and headed down the street again. Eddie didn't answer. She stopped and anxiously turned to him. "She's gone, right? She went back north, didn't she?"

"Naah. She's not gone anywhere, I don't think." He tapped the hat nervously against his knee. "We just didn't think we ought to be walking around asking for trouble, just the two of us, a white boy and a colored girl together, see. I said I thought she ought to wait back at the yard, and she thought so, too. She wanted to stay there. I don't think she likes Atlanta too much."

She sniffed and wiped her nose, wishing he hadn't left Lenora alone, but knowing there was nothing else he could've done. She supposed they'd be leaving Atlanta now, hopping another train that would take them off into the night toward some other city or town. They were walking into the sun and it made her head ache worse, that and the blaring of automobile horns, a pedestrian knocking into her every so often. They passed beneath the huge marquee of the Rialto Theater, where Katharine Hepburn was starring in *Morning Glory*, and then by a small hotel called "The Marquee." A small sign on the door said WHITES ONLY in small, black letters.

The sky behind the red and gray brick buildings was a ribbon of pink as they reached the railroad yard, where rows of wide, hollow piping were strung, end to end on top of the ground. Eddie walked along them, peering inside. "Lenora, Lenora," he called softly. Finally there was a muffled answer. He bent over, tossing his hat aside. "It worked. Look, Lenora, I got Elizabeth back!" Elizabeth squatted down and stuck her head inside. A figure was hunched in the center, like a bundle of clothing rolled into a ball. Emerging from the bundle was a foot, and then Lenora lifted her head.

"Dozed off," she said sleepily. "Elizabeth. You're back. You're back from jail?"

Elizabeth nodded. "Let's go, all right?" She stood and

turned toward Eddie. "I want to catch the next train going."

He studied her face, then solemnly asked, "To where?"

"I don't care," she answered. "Back north. To Pittsburgh or Cleveland or home." She turned and looked toward the tracks.

"Well, all right, but I'm going to see about getting some food first. We're not taking off on empty stomachs. We've seen where *that* gets us."

She shrugged, as if it didn't much matter. It did, but leaving Atlanta mattered more.

"I've got to return this outfit, too. And then we can blow this town for good. If I get stuck or something, you know, just go on without me."

She looked down at his foot drawing circles in the dirt, and imagined the man who owned the suit dragging him through the window by his collar. She stuck her hands into her pockets and took a step toward him. "We won't go without you, will we, Lenora?"

"No," said Lenora.

Standing at the end of the tunnel, it reached them as a series of "no's" strung together.

"Be careful." She reached for his arm, and then he nodded and stepped away into the shadows.

She stood for a minute looking hard at the circle he'd drawn in the dirt, until the spot began to turn colors, green, yellow, and then white, before her eyes.

"Come on down here . . . ere . . . ere . . . ere . . . ere . . ." she heard Lenora say.

It was dark and chilly, and every few minutes the ground would tremble and the tunnel would roar with the din of a freight train steaming out of or into the yard. Curled up against the hard, cold metal, Elizabeth was half afraid that each train leaving would be the last, and they'd have lost their chance to get out of Atlanta forever.

"You sure you don't want to tell me about it?" Lenora asked her again.

"Yes," Elizabeth answered hoarsely, her chin tucked down into her chest. She strained to hear Eddie's footsteps, wanting nothing more than to be asleep inside a freight train again, the wheels rumbling beneath her, the boxcar rocking her side to side. She didn't want to hurt Lenora's feelings, though, so she added, "I just slept because I was sick, and then Eddie came and got me out. That's all, really." She shut her eyes, listening, then thinking, what if she heard footsteps and they weren't Eddie's, and remembering what they'd told her when she left the jail. She shifted position to ease the cramping in her legs.

"Why isn't Eddie back yet?"

"Don't know."

"Hasn't it been enough time now?" she asked again a few minutes later. The way her words echoed made her head feel worse. She hated the sound of fear in her voice.

"He'll be coming any time now, Elizabeth. Stop worrying."

Then she heard Lenora sliding toward her across the tunnel, felt Lenora's arms suddenly around her shoulders, pulling her close. "Maybe that's the worst thing will ever happen to you," Lenora whispered close to her ear. "Think of it like that. That it wasn't a good thing, and you shouldn't have been there, but it's over."

She felt herself go limp, and then her face was wet again, the gentle rocking of Lenora's arms letting her cry.

Eddie returned after the last light outside the tunnel had faded to a purplish black. He'd "run into" someone on the way back to the yard who'd said there were jobs down in Jacksonville.

Some new industry paying good wages had just got going. You couldn't get those jobs, but you might have a chance at the ones folks were leaving to take the new ones. "But I wouldn't blame you for not listening to me," he joked. "Here's a bag of doughnuts, not too stale, I think."

Elizabeth chewed slowly, hungry, but not sure yet what her stomach would take. She knew they were all thinking, weighing their chances. Florida was farther south still. Maybe this lead was their big break, but maybe it meant more trouble.

⇢⇢⇢ 19 ⇠⇠⇠

"IT SEEMS LIKE I'M ON A GIANT FERRIS WHEEL," SIGHED EDDIE, "going round and round, and every time I stop and try to get off and stay somewhere for a while, I have to get back on again. I've got motion sickness from going in circles, not getting anywhere where I can plant my feet for good for a while. Know what I mean?"

"Yeah," said Lenora. "Afraid I do."

Elizabeth nodded. She wouldn't have wanted to hear him talk like that before, would have preferred he knew just where they were headed and why, even if he had to pretend. But she was used to it now. Nothing had come easy and nothing would.

A brown beetle carefully inched its way up a wooden slat as though it were certain of *its* destination. Elizabeth rolled over on a sack of flour, on which she'd had her best night's sleep in a boxcar. They had been riding all night on a slow-moving train. Elizabeth had awakened once and shook Lenora awake.

"What, what?" cried Lenora. "What's wrong? Stop crying, I can't understand you."

Elizabeth had dreamed she was riding a train through a tunnel down into the ground. There weren't any trains going back, and there was no light anywhere.

"Go back to sleep, Elizabeth." Lenora patted her head. "Forget about Atlanta."

Now Lenora had the door open and was sitting with her legs dangling over the side. "I never seen so many filling stations and ads for pecans," she said.

Eddie rose, brushed off his overalls, and went to stand behind her. "Funny how things turn out," he was saying. "See, when I was younger I pictured myself going around to all these cities on a train, sort of like we're doing now. I was going to be a ballplayer, you know, like Ruth and Gehrig. Going by train from ballpark to ballpark. New York, Detroit, Philadelphia, Chicago. . . . The dreams you have when you're a kid, geez. Look at all those trees. Sure pretty here, isn't it?"

"What would you have been, Eddie, a pitcher?" Elizabeth asked, looking up at him.

"I played second in a sandlot league," he said, turning to smile at her. "Well, if we get to Florida and have to pick oranges, maybe it won't be so bad. They're about the size of baseballs. Get my throwing arm back in shape so I'll be ready case this trouble ever ends. Here, Elizabeth, you catch. Squat down, like this."

"I know how to catch," she replied, bending her knees. She held up an imaginary mitt and two fingers for a signal. He shook his head and waited for another, then gripped an imaginary ball behind his back and wound up to throw.

"In there, baby, for an O and one count. Maybe I *could* be a pitcher." As he went into motion again, Elizabeth jumped to her feet and swung a make-believe bat. "A towering drive," she said, looking off into the distance. "It's GONE!"

"I thought you were on my team!"

She shrugged and smiled.

"C'mon, give a guy a break!" he pleaded.

"The only good thing about going farther south is we don't need coats," said Lenora. "Otherwise, I wouldn't be going."

"Yeah." Eddie dropped to the floor beside her. "At least we won't be like one of those stiffs they find frozen in a boxcar up north. You go to sleep and don't wake up. Boxcar nothing. In winter they're iceboxes, traveling tombs."

Elizabeth picked up the map. "If we'd gone a different way, through Tallahassee, we could've passed through Two Egg and Buck's Siding. Two *eggs*," she mused dreamily as they pulled into the Jacksonville yard, "and a side of bacon. Wouldn't that be something?"

She thought, after a half-day wandering around Jacksonville, that in some ways it looked like Cleveland, Pittsburgh, and all the other cities they'd passed through: boarded-up store-fronts, "going-out-of-business" sales, soup lines, flophouses, the benches in the park all taken. In other ways, it was nothing like the others, with flowers blooming so late in fall, palm trees fringing the town square, huge ocean liners and banana and shrimp boats lined up at the docks. All Eddie could talk about was how warm it was, and she reminded him that they hadn't come to Florida for a vacation.

They spent the first few nights in the basement of a Catholic church, where they were allowed three nights' stay. Along with the free noon meals, they were given the addresses of the local employment offices and the bus and train stations.

She went off the first morning on her own, hitting the

employment office first thing. Inside, she stood on the tips of her toes, craning her neck to see over the throng clustered in front of the bulletin board like a crowd storming the gates at a baseball park, only subdued in its defeated silence. She began to wedge her way up front, trading a sharp jab in the ribs now and then for a better view.

"Hey, missy! Look where you're steppin'."

She'd shifted her weight from one foot to another and landed on someone's toe. In backing away she'd trounced on someone else's. She could hardly turn her head without some person thinking she was rude. She drew her feet and arms and both hands in close and peered around the brim of the man's hat in front of her.

"Hey, take your hat off," someone shouted from behind. Once he did, Elizabeth could see the board clearly, several typed announcements on three-by-five cards under a heading called "Domestic Work" and all the empty space in between. It was right then that she also saw Vera.

She was a row or two in front and a little off to the right, so that Elizabeth caught just a slice of her profile. For several moments she stood there astounded, wondering what could have brought Vera to Florida. Had her mother died after all, or had she come looking for Elizabeth? But how could she have known where she was? Then joy welled up inside her, propelling her through the crowd, so that she was hardly aware of the elbows thrown her way.

"Vera! Vera!" She knew Vera couldn't hear, because of a staticky announcement from a loudspeaker. Now half the mob had turned and were pushing their way toward the job desk. She kept forging ahead, getting stepped on and run into, until finally she was close to the bulletin board and to Vera. *"Vera!"*

She threw her arms around Vera's neck, but the woman

wrenched herself out of Elizabeth's grip and backed herself against the board. Elizabeth gasped and stepped back herself. The woman was at least twenty years older than Vera, her dark hair streaked with charcoal gray, her eyes big with astonishment.

"Oh, oh, I'm sorry," said Elizabeth, her hands dropping to her sides.

The woman eased herself slowly along the wall and out of Elizabeth's reach, then hurried across the room.

"Vera," she whispered to herself, before she turned back to the board, feeling crushed. The crowd was swelling all around her again. After a while, she read the cards on the board herself, rereading them several times, until she'd accepted she wouldn't qualify as a horse trainer, bricklayer, or rabbi. She pushed through the crowd and out the front door.

She walked aimlessly for several blocks, feeling foolish and sad, afraid and lonely. She was in yet another city with nowhere to go and nothing to do, and she was hungry again. When she came to Bay Street she stopped. A long line had formed in front of a bakery. Gulls swooped overhead and pigeons hunted crumbs on the sidewalk. Florida was *hot,* she realized, wiping her forehead. As she attached herself to the end of the line, the woman in front of her turned and smiled.

"It's the best bread in town. You'll see."

Elizabeth nodded and smiled back at the friendly face.

"They make it with whiskey."

"Really? Whiskey?" she said, watching a gull flying low.

"You know soda bread?"

She nodded again, staring at her feet. She didn't feel like talking, and the line would be a slow one.

"It's almost like that. But whiskey. Mr. Lyon himself pipes it in from outer space."

Elizabeth looked up. The woman's eyes shone like glints of blue-green glass.

"Look, here comes a shipment now." She pointed to a cement truck crawling down the street. "I used to drive a rig like that. We shipped babies all around the world. Some still were sucking, know what I mean? Yer too young. We'd give 'em whiskey. Har! My baby was a nigger baby. I'm not colored, but the devil is. That's how nigger babies get to be born."

Elizabeth took a step back, as the woman stepped toward her, laughing in silence, widening a mouth with no teeth. She smiled and ran her tongue along the whitened edge of a pale pink gum.

"Do you listen to the radio?"

Elizabeth nodded again, still stepping backward.

"Don't." The woman had left her place in line, was following Elizabeth and wagging her finger. "Once I turned the radio off and the devil talked to me the whole night anyway. Had to throw it out the window. Came in on the pipeline, too. You've got to watch out. Soda bread, c'mon. Are you Irish?"

Elizabeth stepped backward off the curb and fell into the street. The woman extended a filthy, gnarled hand and Elizabeth got up and ran.

When she stopped running she found herself in front of a flat, white building behind a metal fence overlooking a river. Above a set of double doors a sign said OFFICE. She stood staring and then shrugged her shoulders and went inside. "I've got nothing to lose," she thought.

The office was dimly lit, like out of some novel she'd read by Dickens. She was still out of breath when she entered and asked the woman behind a desk about work. The woman picked up her phone and a man came out of another inner office, into which he ushered Elizabeth. It was funny she should come in just then, he said, because a girl had just quit. Did she know how to sew? How was her eyesight, and could she follow instructions? Had she had TB or other illnesses? Tardiness was not permitted

149

under any circumstances, nor was talking on the job. She left with instructions to report to work at seven the next morning.

Later, Elizabeth unrolled a mattress, which smelled of sweat and disinfectant, and lay down on the church basement floor. Studying the ceiling, she told herself she could learn to sew on a machine; she could learn to do anything. She would send a note to her family right away.

Eddie had told her to make sure the shop wasn't a front for something else, "like gangland stuff." She said she was sure it was on the up-and-up, but she would be careful.

"Hey," Lenora whispered now. "You look and see if there are other colored working there, and if there are you be sure and tell me."

She promised Lenora she would.

⇢⟫ 20 ⟪⇠

A LIGHT RAIN WAS FALLING AS SHE HURRIED UP THE CHURCH STEPS to the sidewalk the next morning. Taking the steps two at a time, she wondered now if she'd invented the whole story about getting a job as she'd invented Vera or maybe caught some craziness from the woman in the breadline. She didn't like the feeling of going off on her own without Eddie or Lenora, either. She wished she could take them with her. But she'd go *anywhere* alone for eight cents an hour. At ten hours a day for six days, that was more than her pa was making when she'd left.

She'd awakened when the town whistle, Big Jim, went off before dawn, but she was still afraid she'd be late on the first day and lose the job before she started. Instead, she arrived too early and had to wait a half hour until the gate opened at 6:45. When finally it swung open, she felt frozen with fear and let a dozen women stream by her before she stepped inside herself.

Once Elizabeth was inside the factory, a hefty woman wearing a badge gave her a blue smock to wear over her trousers. "Get yourself a skirt," she told her. "Trousers won't do." Then she was led to a work station near the middle of a large, low-ceilinged room in which rows and rows of females, all white, sat motionless at black machines, as though waiting for a teacher to enter a classroom. But at seven o'clock on the nose all the machines started to whir and drone at once, like a roomful of giant mechanical bees.

Elizabeth sat down, clasping with both hands a small brown lunch bag given to her by one of the nuns.

"The best way to keep your job," a young girl at the next table whispered, "is to stay bent over your machine the whole day. Rule number one is never draw attention to yourself."

"But no one's showed me what to do," Elizabeth whispered back, looking anxiously around. The piece of equipment before her looked like a monstrous contraption, not like her mother's small Singer.

"Don't worry," the girl replied, giving her a steady, serious look. "He'll be by."

Elizabeth waited on the stool in front of her machine, her uneasiness mounting as the minutes passed. She was a fool for thinking she could learn how to sew. She knew nothing about sewing machines except what she'd seen of her mother pedaling away in a corner of the kitchen. Her hands would not work; they were trembling and cold.

"You the new girl?"

She jumped, because he'd come up behind her.

"Yes," she replied, holding onto the bag tightly so that he would not see her trembling. He was short and squat like a bulldog, with steel gray eyes. "Can you sew a straight line?" he asked. She thought it was a joke and laughed politely. He stared at her grimly, not blinking. She dropped her lunch bag to the floor, and he said to carry it over to the lunchroom.

"It's rules we have to keep them there," the same girl later whispered. "But try not to let yours be on the bottom. Rats."

She spent the whole day learning how to run her machine, making mistakes and starting over, pulling out the thread and beginning again and again. She remembered her elation of the night before and wondered why she'd been so happy. By mid-afternoon every nerve and muscle pleaded with her to get up and move. But she'd already gone to the rest room once. And she'd heard more talk about the foreman at lunch. She imagined his eyes on her the rest of the afternoon and told herself she was making things up in her head, just to go on sewing. Once she looked up and there he was, staring from where he leaned against the concrete wall, dragging on a cigarette. She jabbed her finger and ran a seam crooked as the Mississippi River.

She went back to the church that night and told Lenora and Eddie she was quitting. The work was too hard and her back ached. It was harder by far than picking tobacco. They had saved her some soup and bread from lunch and they watched silently while she ate it cold. She fell asleep quickly and slept soundly but awoke when Big Jim went off the next morning.

"I can't do it," she thought, pulling the blanket up past her chin. She closed her eyes and tried to fall back asleep. Someone was snoring. A horn tooted outside, and footsteps thumped on the ceiling above. Creeping out from under the blanket, Elizabeth tiptoed around the bodies strewn about the floor across to the bathroom to wash up. She couldn't afford to be late.

Lenora and Eddie were waiting for her outside the gate. She was bone tired and hungry again, but there was nothing to do but start walking and looking. They had used up their three nights at the church and had to move on.

The neighborhood around the factory was full of abandoned

153

buildings and warehouses, and they soon discovered that some were easy to enter by way of broken windows or doors that were easily forced. By six o'clock they'd moved into the old office of the Perfect Pest Control Service and Eddie went out looking for food. He was back in an hour with a bag of overripened fruit and a small cut under his left eye. "The things you have to fight for," he said, shaking his head.

But the Perfect Pest Control office was so full of vermin they moved out the next day.

The alleyway between the two small wooden buildings was narrow, and it took some maneuvering to pull herself up onto the window ledge and force the window open. Elizabeth stuck her head inside and sniffed, the same way she entered a strange boxcar. The place didn't smell great, like a basement closed up all winter, with maybe a layer of year-old grease over everything. She motioned with her hand for them to follow, as she dropped to the floor and sent a bucket or something clattering with her foot.

She pulled a book of matches from her pocket and struck one, lighting a large wad of paper in her hand, which sent shadows streaking across the dark room. Two walls were lined with mostly empty shelves, another with a tall metal cabinet. Wooden crates were strewn about the floor, and to her left was a set of swinging doors, which she edged toward with Eddie and Lenora following behind.

The other room wasn't as dark, strips of light from a street lamp seeping through spaces in the boarded-up front window. Elizabeth held the torch away from her body, casting light on a row of booths hugging one side of the room. Along the opposite wall were a row of stools, a counter, and behind the counter two refrigerators, a sink, a long grill, an oven, and a large menu board

154

on the wall. She hurried across the room and tossed the burning paper down into the sink, dropping the room into near darkness again.

"Huh. It's a *restaurant,*" said Eddie. "I'll be damned." He stood for a minute, scanning the place wrapped in shadows, then walked over to one of the booths and ran his hand lightly across the table top. "We had a place like this called 'Little Al's' we used to go to sometimes in Kokomo, especially after basketball games. That's what it reminds me of. Same color tables and all. Gee."

"Looks like a lotta places I been to." Lenora hitched her skirt up higher and rested her hands on her hips. "Do you suppose it was for 'whites only,' or what?"

"So what?" Elizabeth turned to flash Lenora a look of mutual indignation, then went over to the row of stools and slid onto one of them, resting her head on the cool marble counter. Morning would come in no time. She could not put in another day's work without a decent night's sleep, but that seemed impossible without even a blanket. "I'd stay anywhere tonight, vermin or not," she sighed, "I'm so tired. Let's eat whatever we have and go to sleep."

"Sure," said Eddie. "You talk brave, but I remember you last night, scrambling up onto that desk to get away from those little critters. You would've been inside one of those drawers if they were big enough to hold you." He laughed, drifting toward the front window, and stooped to pick up a rag from a pile in the corner.

"I would've been inside it with her, and so would you." Lenora crossed the room to stand beside her. "Look, Elizabeth, don't fall asleep with your head on the counter. A cockroach might mistake it for a hamburger."

"Look," said Eddie.

Elizabeth lifted her head. He'd rubbed off the soot from the inside of the front window and stepped back to read it. The faded red letters said:

Dora's
Coming Home Cafe

"Well, I guess we're home then," said Lenora, rubbing her eyes and yawning. "I wonder who Dora was."

→⟩⟩ 21 ⟨⟨←

ELIZABETH WAS HALFWAY HOME, WALKING THE SIX BLOCKS FROM the shop to the cafe as she did every night, with a sense of freedom and anticipation. The streets in the neighborhood were nearly always deserted. The darkness and chill in the air only added to the pleasure of catching a first glimpse of the yellow light glowing behind the boarded-up window.

A wiry orange tomcat leaped across her path as she stepped up onto a curb and turned a corner. Then it turned to scold her from atop a porch railing, wailing as she passed it by. "Poor, poor Tom," she crooned.

She was glad for the six-block walk because it gave her time in which to think at the end of each day. After two weeks, she'd grown slightly more comfortable in her job, facing the broad, flat pieces of cotton at her machine each day almost as if they were old friends, drawing some satisfaction from the joining together of two halves of material into one. Running the needle down one seam after another, she seemed to forget about her problems, as though nothing mattered but getting the seams straight. Still, she couldn't imagine how somebody could do this kind of work her whole life. But, judging from the way the workers had been disappearing from their jobs, maybe nobody did. A girl could be at her station one day and then gone the next, as if a giant hand had descended from the sky to whisk her away. It happened a lot. Lately, she'd overheard whispered conversations at lunch about unions and began to suspect that it was all connected. She didn't like to think about it, but she supposed it all had something to do with how she came to get the job in the first place. Maybe some poor girl had been fired, maybe even one with a kid. She remembered her father talking about unions when he still had his Pullman job, but she couldn't recall what he'd said.

She passed in front of the only grocery in the neighborhood still open for business and stopped to read the crudely hand-lettered signs about pork butts, lettuce, and skimmed milk on butcher paper taped to the window. She would have loved to bring home something special, a surprise for Eddie and Lenora but didn't know if she ought to. Four dollars and eighty cents a week had sounded like a monstrous sum of money at first, but neither Eddie nor Lenora had found regular work. Now and then Eddie picked up an odd job by hanging around the docks, helping fishermen unload their boats, sweeping up for a foreman once in a while inside a warehouse. Sometimes they paid him in fish, and he came home with a piece of cod or a few of the smaller shrimp for dinner. Once in a while he'd pick up some change or even a buck. Lenora earned a nickel here and there from someone she met at a colored church, feeding the woman's invalid uncle his lunch.

Elizabeth sighed and kept on walking. They all needed shoes and socks and a million other things, but what about coats for her brothers? She couldn't imagine Mrs. *Roosevelt* had sent some. Nor did she expect her father had got more work. She swallowed hard, thinking of Waldo going to school in a coat that left his bony little wrists exposed to the cold. If she could somehow send half the money home, it surely would help. And then after three months, a raise.

She knew Eddie and Lenora would have given anything to be in her shoes with a regular job. She knew they got by eating as little as they could, unless it was something they'd gotten hold of themselves. As it was, they were always out hunting for work and food and other things they all needed. Eddie was so proud the day he came home with the old kerosene lamp, given to him by a nice man at the docks. And the same woman with the invalid uncle gave Lenora a hot plate, which they were able to use because Eddie had some mysterious way of flipping the electricity on. . . . It was amazing what a little light and heated-up food had done for their spirits.

She slipped into the shadows alongside the cafe, lifted the window, and pulled herself up onto the ledge.

"I like it when you come home at night. It's sorta like you're the dad." Lenora rested her chin in her hand and smiled at Elizabeth, swatting a two-inch cockroach scurrying across the table.

"So what does that make *me*, Lenora? If Elizabeth's the dad, who am I?" Eddie stirred the contents of the pot with a big wooden spoon, then used a rag to lift it off the hot plate, coming around from behind the counter.

"We run out of things to talk about, Eddie and me." Lenora dropped her voice to a whisper. "And I always beat him in cards. Even when he cheats. He's not very good."

"What are you telling her?" said Eddie. He stood in front

of the table, holding the pot, his white apron smudged and stained. They'd been lucky, finding the apron, along with some pots, pans, dishes, silverware, a game of checkers, some dog food, toothpaste, and two frayed novels in cabinets back in the storeroom. "Our special tonight is beans with ham hock. Would you care for some? Good." He dipped the ladle into the pot and smiled at Elizabeth.

"Wait." Elizabeth pointed to the menu board still posted behind the counter, listing dozens of entries. "I'll have that meat loaf special, instead. Please."

"What?" He turned and gave her an incredulous look. "The meat loaf? Naah. You don't want that. Our meat loaf is dry and crusty." He mimicked a scowl and shook his head.

"Well, I don't want it if it's dry and crusty. I suppose the BLT would be okay instead, then. And please toast the bread." She pretended a fake condescending smile.

"Oh, gosh, no," he said. "The lettuce is all icky brown at the edges, and the tomato is mushy. Look at these beans, though." He shoved the pot under her nose. "See, red ones and yellow ones both. And look at the size of that ham hock! We grow our own beans, too, out in the back yard."

"And the ham hock?" asked Lenora.

"Well—she was just a stray, sort of had run of the neighborhood. But I heard she came from good stock, Indiana, I think."

"Oooh, all right," Elizabeth sighed, heaving her shoulders. "Give me some of that stuff, then."

He smiled, dishing beans onto the three white plates on the table, and slid in beside Lenora. "Tough customers, you two. You know, if I could somehow get the gas on, that stove and grill would work. We could open this place up for lunch."

"Oh, sure, without a license." Lenora rolled her eyes, reaching for a piece of bread. "We'd be in jail in no time. It's enough you got the electricity on, and I don't want to know how you did it."

"Maybe the city wouldn't find out."

"Somebody probably owns this place, don't forget," Lenora went on. "And she could pop in any second and we'd be gone before you know it."

"Lenora and I made these beans together. We do everything together. Good, huh?" He winked at Elizabeth and lifted a spoonful to his mouth.

She smiled and went on eating. They were used to her not talking much at night. She just liked to listen and eat and go to bed early. Sometimes Eddie would come home late, after she and Lenora had eaten, and Lenora would talk—about husband Jim and baby Rebecca, her ma and her aunts and uncles and cousins, about growing up in Philadelphia, and moving to New York when she was twelve. Elizabeth only knew Lenora as a friend and companion, but she tried to imagine Lenora in her other life, as a mother, as some mother's daughter. She liked to hear her stories, except when Lenora talked about going back some day to start over.

"I been trying to see in my mind that recipe book I had on the kitchen counter, so I could remember some more recipes, now that we got a way to heat things," said Lenora, squinting as if she were trying to look backward in time. "If we ever did get the oven going, I'd make us a meat loaf you'd die for."

"I'm ready," said Eddie. "Just give me that meat loaf and bury me six feet under."

". . . full of onions and bacon and catsup. . . . I can smell it now, yes I can. . . . Did you ever think . . . ?" Lenora put her spoon down and leaned her head back, closing her eyes. "Life wasn't easy then, not at all. But you get used to it being a certain way, and you think it'll go on the same way forever. We had our colored depression long before yours, but when yours came ours got worse. I mean, look at us here. Could you ever have thought this up?" She looked from Elizabeth to Eddie and with a gesture of her hand took in the whole room.

"At least we got roots here now, not just blowin' around in the wind, like something cut loose. . . ." said Eddie.

"Yes," said Lenora. "That's right." She reached for Elizabeth's hand, which held her spoon in midair. "Hey, wake up. Aren't you hungry?"

With effort, Elizabeth opened her eyes. "Hungry, yes," she replied, trying to hold her head up.

"Poor thing," said Lenora, patting her arm.

"I'd feel bad if I thought you didn't like your dinner," said Eddie.

"It's really good. See? I'm eating it now." Elizabeth raised her fork to her mouth and closed her eyes, feigning sleep.

"Go ahead, keep it up, and see who does the dishes." He nudged her foot under the table. "I wish it was me being that tired. I really do. But I'm going to keep hanging out at the docks. Something's bound to break and I'll get a lead—maybe for both of us, Lenora."

"Sure, you find me a job, Eddie." There wasn't a trace of faith in her voice.

"Someday when you're not so tired, you come down to the docks with me, Elizabeth. You liked it, didn't you, Lenora?"

"Yes, all those handsome colored men unloading those boats, singing with their shirts off. . . ."

"They hoist the bananas to the pier in these huge nets," Eddie went on. "This one guy told me not to feel bad I got paid in fish. He said he used to get paid in bananas and to this day he can't eat a banana unless it's hidden in Jell-O or something."

"You shouldn't feel bad," said Elizabeth. "We need the fish.

162

It helps us a lot." Then she smiled, remembering how her mother had taken her and Waldo to a fair at Navy Pier downtown, back home in Chicago. She told them about it, recalling how they "went aboard the ship and Waldo and I were so impressed with the starched white uniforms and black polished shoes we both decided we were going to be sailors."

"The dreams you have when you're a kid," said Eddie.

"Here, Elizabeth," said Lenora, reaching around to the table behind them. "There's a little library in the church basement and I took a book out for you. It's some sort of mystery."

She thanked Lenora and got up from the table. The mattresses they'd retrieved from a junkyard were stacked against a wall, and she pulled one down onto the floor and reached for her sweater. With her back to the wall, she opened the book to the first page.

"It'd be nice to have a radio someday," she heard Eddie say. "Maybe I could pick up something broken and fix it."

"And maybe a small rug," said Lenora. "I haven't seen one anywhere, though, not even at the dump."

Elizabeth didn't want to fall asleep right away, because if she did, then it would be morning all over again. So she drifted through that narrow place between sleep and consciousness marked by a slight whirring in the ears. It was softer than a sewing machine, more like the hum of an electric refrigerator.

"Look at her," said Lenora. "Falling asleep and it ain't eight o'clock."

"Yea," said Eddie. "But I wish it were me so tired from working all the time."

"You're working more'n me."

"I know. I feel bad you can't get anything."

"I don't even feel all right going out for a walk in this neighborhood."

"Don't start talking about going back again, Lenora. Please? Nobody will bother you around here if you . . ."

"Stay in my place. I know."

"I was going to say 'if you're careful.' It's not all that different up north. Just a different sort of rules."

"You're just afraid if I go, she'll follow me back, ain't you?"

"That's not the only reason," he said. "*I* want you here, too. If I didn't like you, you'd know it by now, don't you think?"

"You like her a lot, don't you?"

"Sure, and I like you, too."

"Not *that* way, though. I can see it in your eyes, Eddie, how they follow her around. You can hide it from her, but not from me. . . ."

"Want to play cards?"

"No. Let's get these dishes done."

Elizabeth started and tried to open her eyes, but her head fell forward again. She ought to go to bed so she wouldn't have trouble getting up for school. Who was it that was doing all that talking? The voices she heard were familiar, but she wasn't sure who it was. If it was Waldo wanting her to play cards, she was just too tired. She ought instead to get up and clear off the table, but she suddenly felt confused. Instead of the kitchen table she saw in her mind a booth, with green upholstery and a gray tabletop. The faraway voices went on and she strained to listen:

". . . and what if somebody suddenly said the Depression was over. There were now jobs and places to live and plenty of money for everyone. Where would you go?"

"It's hard to imagine," said Eddie, "its ever being over."

"You know, I was wrong about you," said Lenora. "At first I thought you was wild, after only one thing and pleasing yourself. You're just a small-town boy caught in a big-time mess. You're scared like everyone. You learn to act tough and brave and cocky when all you feel is scared and alone."

There was a long silence. They were familiar voices again, but Elizabeth still wasn't sure whose. She tried to open her eyes, but her head fell forward onto the open book.

"I know what I would do," said Lenora. "If the Depression was over, I'd go back to New York and start over. Get a regular job and buy a little house with a yard full of grass and flowers. Maybe find somebody to love again some day. I dream about things like that, especially the yard and grass and flowers. The things I want are soft, like a new baby's skin and a soft blanket underneath her. A carpet to step onto in the morning when the floors are cold. A warm hand on my back, waking me up nice and gentlelike. . . ."

"I still dream about grass, too," said Eddie. "Only it's in a ballpark."

Elizabeth was dreaming that there was music coming from the abandoned Harmony Piano and Organ store across the street, and when she went inside she found her father selling radios. There were rows and rows of them all lined up on a marble counter like the one in the Hollywood Grill on Michigan Avenue, and they were all white like the Philco at home. Home. But she *was* home, wasn't she? In the dream, her father rushed to greet her, engulfing her in his arms. "You've come home, *ja!*" Then all the radios started playing a song in Swedish, and they were all around the kitchen table again, her ma and pa, Waldo and Whitney, and they were laughing and singing and swaying along with the music.

➤➤ 22 ◀◀

ELIZABETH COUGHED AND FANNED THE NEWSPAPER IN FRONT OF her face. "Eddie, that thing really stinks!"

"Okay, I'm sorry."

"You could at least blow it the other direction."

He was leaning against the wall, puffing on a long, fat cigar, his legs outstretched on the cushioned seat of the booth. "Well, I got paid today for sweeping up at the King Edward Cigar factory and they gave me a half dozen. Did you know that cigar makers had the first union ever in Florida?"

"Really?" she said absently. "No, I never heard that." She folded the note to her parents around two dollar bills and placed it in the envelope. Hard as she tried, she was still unable to save much money, needing a couple of blouses and another skirt for work, and there was always food to buy. Food, food, *food.* It never ended. She looked at Eddie's cigar and sighed. It *would* be nice if he got paid in cash more often. It would be nice, too, if she were making ten cents an hour as the union wanted, but she was afraid to risk her job and go to meetings.

"A lot of the workers were from Cuba, and they started one when they migrated. . . . Maybe I ought to be a teacher. I think I know a lot about a lot of things."

"I don't know if that's such a good idea. Vera's father is a high school teacher and he went a long time without getting paid at all. They lost their house because of it."

"Yeah," he said, holding the cigar between two fingers. "Well, maybe they should've had a union."

She pulled part of the *Sentinel* toward her and began to tear the page down the middle. "I don't see what difference it makes if there's no money to pay them."

"No money, hah!" He leaned toward her with his elbows on the table. "Did you know your city was paying Sally Rand something like six thousand dollars a week to dance at your Fair?"

She remembered her father ranting about dancers at the Fair and blushed. "No," she replied, "I didn't."

He leaned closer. "And did you know the name 'Chicago' comes from the Indian phrase 'shika'ko'? It means 'skunk place.' " He laughed and slipped the cigar between his teeth.

"What's *that* got to do with anything? Anyhow, *this* is a skunk place." She picked up the newspaper and fanned it furiously.

"What's that you're sending them from the paper?"

"The column by Mrs. Roosevelt, in case my ma missed it. It's about how she faces her problems when they seem insurmountable." She licked the envelope and sealed it shut.

"When things were getting bad for us, my dad used to clip articles from the paper and leave them on the kitchen table so we would see them. The stories would be about the unemployment rates around the country, and how tough times were for most

167

people. He did it so we would know it wasn't his fault, that it was that bad for almost everyone. Poor Pa. Say, you know who's kept their jobs, who's not out of work, don't you?"

"No," she replied, glancing up at him. "Who?"

"Movie stars. They're makin' movies like crazy these days. Maybe instead of teaching I could go into movies. Look at me closely, don't I remind you of anyone?" He slowly exhaled a curl of white smoke.

"Yeah, a mobster, a G-man."

"I don't remind you of someone you've seen in the movies?"

"Mickey Rooney?" she guessed with a teasing smile. "Groucho Marx?"

"Awww, c'mon."

"Well, I don't know. Who then?" She leaned back into the seat and waited.

He grinned and pushed his hat back. "I was thinking Clark Gable."

She tilted her head and examined him. "I don't think so, Eddie. I can't really see it."

"I was going to say you looked a little like Greta Garbo yourself, but now I won't." He chomped down on the cigar and folded his arms across his chest.

"Well, now, wait a second. Maybe you could get into movies and just play yourself. Did you ever think of that?" She refolded the newspaper and pushed it aside, smiling across the table.

He pulled the cigar from his mouth and studied her face. She looked away, feeling suddenly awkward.

"There's something about you now. You've changed."

"Have I?" she said, running her hand self-consciously through her hair.

"Yeah. You're not that sniveling kid in that train back in Chicago, crying to take you with me, and then crying to go back home. You're a lot more sure of yourself."

She spread her hands out flat on the tabletop and studied her nails. "Well, I don't feel sure of myself most of the time."

"It's honest of you to admit that, but I still say you're not like you were."

"No, I suppose not." She thought back to the time he was talking about, remembering how terrified she'd felt. It was true; she didn't feel like that anymore. "But," she said aloud, "usually I feel like a scared kid out in the big world, and what am I doing out in it, anyway? I should be back in school, but here I am. . . ."

"Well, you keep plowing ahead and I like that. Going off every day by yourself to a real hard job, and you're so young. It takes nerve. Did you ever see that movie where Katharine Hepburn plays a pilot—"

"Yes! *Christopher Strong!*" she interrupted. "You saw it, too?"

"Yeah, I was working in Kansas City then, so I could afford a movie once in a while. I remember Hepburn up in that plane, pulling off that oxygen mask and taking that plane up higher and higher. She was pregnant, you know. That's why she did it."

"*I* know. I saw it, Eddie."

"And she dies so her lover isn't ruined. I remember her in that black beret and out in that boat, telling him she could never love anyone but him. And then she says something like, 'Being in love with a reckless person like me wouldn't suit you at all.' "

She traced a crack in the palm of her hand with her fingernail. "I think I saw it the day I met you down by the tracks. I remember, because when I was thinking of leaving home later that night, I remembered her up in that plane, and I thought if somebody could do *that,* then I could face what I had to do."

"I like girls with nerve. That's why I sat through it twice. It must mean something that you saw it the day you met me, don't you think?" He watched the smoke curl upward above his head.

"I don't know. Maybe," she said. She picked up the pencil and twirled it between her fingers, keeping her head down.

"Yep, you've really grown up some. I guess you'll just keep getting older and more mature all the time now, maybe even have a family some day. All of that kind of grown-up stuff."

She looked up into his eyes. "I haven't thought so far ahead, Eddie. Sometimes, though, it seems like I already *have* a family. Back home, you know. I guess it's odd to feel that way, but . . . anyway, I've never even had a date." She felt the color inching up her neck and into her face.

"Yeah, well . . ." He moistened his lips and went on. "Well, if I was at your high school, I would've asked you for a date by now." His voice broke, collapsing into a croak, and he covered his mouth and coughed.

Elizabeth's gaze followed the pencil as it traced a crack in the counter. "That's really nice of you, Eddie."

"Do you think you would've gone out with me?" he asked huskily.

She thought for a minute and then nodded.

He smiled. "It's funny to think like that now, isn't it?"

"Yes," she agreed, "it is."

He threw his arm over the back of the booth. "Say, Elizabeth, do you think *I'm* the reckless type?"

She leaned forward, resting her chin in her hand, and smiled. "Yes, I think you're sort of that type."

He lowered his head and shook it, squeezing his eyes shut.

"What's wrong, Eddie?"

"I'm dizzy."

He raised his head and opened his eyes and she saw that his face had turned green. "You don't look well."

Leaning forward, he pressed the stub of the cigar into an empty cup. "I think I better lie down."

"Yeah, you better." She tapped the pencil on the table as she watched him squeeze out of the booth and stumble through the swinging door to the back room. Then she sat for a long while thinking, wondering how it was she could feel happy and sad all at once.

→≫ 23 ≪←

THEY BOWED THEIR HEADS FOR THE BLESSING, WHICH LENORA
bestowed. " 'He hath filled the hungry with good things; and the
rich he hath sent empty away.' Amen."

The table was spread with a roast chicken and dressing from
the pastor's wife at Lenora's church, mashed potatoes, black
beans, green salad, and a store-bought sweet potato pie.

"Of course," said Lenora, reaching for a knife and rising to
carve the bird, "I don't mean the rich any harm, especially on
Christmas." She made a first, neat incision behind the front right
thigh, the rust-colored juice spurting free and trickling down onto
the plate.

"Isn't that about the prettiest sight you ever saw?" said
Eddie. "Last year I was setting pins in a bowling alley in Louis-
ville, living in a lean-to on an empty lot. We roasted apples and
popcorn over a fire and I thought *that* was tops."

"I must've slept through it," said Lenora. "I don't remember
last year."

They both looked at Elizabeth. She was studying the plate of dark meat and white, trying to decide.

"I guess you wish you were home," said Lenora, reaching for the potatoes.

"Sure, I miss them," she replied, turning to glance at Lenora beside her. She reached for Lenora's hand and squeezed it, because she didn't want her to think she wasn't cared about. She was, and so was Eddie. But it *was* Christmas, and she couldn't help remembering.

" 'Course you miss them," said Eddie. "I still miss mine. And you know what else? When the holidays come, I almost wish I were a kid again. It's something that seems to come over me." He was bent over his potatoes, molding them into stiff, white peaks. "I always get nostalgic, you know. I remember things like the time my brothers and I took Ma's ironing board out to the hill behind the school after it snowed. Turned over, it made a great bobsled, but my sister Clara snitched." He laughed.

"The year I got a sled it hardly snowed at all," said Elizabeth. She took the salad from Lenora. "The biggest snowfall was the day I went back to school after Christmas vacation. Thought somebody was playing a mean trick on me."

After dinner they exchanged presents—pieces of fresh fruit, a hunk of real chocolate, socks—around a small tree they got for nothing from Lenora's church. They'd trimmed the tree with labels from cans cut into stars and snowflakes. A tin can angel gleamed down at them from the top.

Elizabeth and Eddie went to an evening church service with Lenora so she didn't have to go alone on Christmas, and to personally thank the pastor's wife for the roast chicken.

She'd never been almost the only white person in a room full of Negroes. She didn't know it would feel like being, once again, in another country, nor that there were so many shades of brown. It was nothing like any service she'd been to before. "Lutherans

173

don't bang on tambourines and fall on the floor," she told Lenora later.

"I've heard that," said Lenora. "And I've heard not all colored do, either."

December 29 was a Friday, cool and drizzly, the sky a muted lavender gray. Running to work because she'd overslept, Elizabeth entered the shop just as the buzzer went off and hurried down the center aisle to her station. Then she stuffed Eddie's pants under her machine and sat down. The girl next to her winked and smiled in a conspiratorial way.

Getting to know the other girls was what made the job bearable, that and the money and having a place to go every day. She didn't like working the long hours in a dimly lit place full of rats. But she could stand it. Her eyes fixed on the cotton all day; she sometimes seemed to lapse into a trance and could see almost forgotten patterns of her own life: the grain of the wood in her family's dining room table, the big patchwork squares of red and blue and yellow on her quilted bedspread, the fraying sleeves on her mother's blue bathrobe, the round, pink rug on Vera's old bedroom floor, the initials carved into her desk at school. . . .

Elizabeth bent over to retrieve Eddie's pants from under her machine. He'd torn them badly vaulting a fence. It was nearly five and a good time to fix them because the bosses all hung around the office, eager to get going. She was starving herself. She slipped the overalls under the needle and depressed the pedal with her foot. She'd mended Lenora's skirt the same way, and the sleeve of her own jacket.

"What's that you've got there?"

The foreman exhaled, a mist of blue-gray smoke dropping over her head like a net. Her knees shook and her hands began to tremble. "I said, 'What have you got there?' " He dropped the butt and ground it into the floor with his toe.

Elizabeth removed Eddie's pants from under the needle and reached for a piece of the shop's navy blue corduroy.

"Don't bother," he hissed. "Pick up your pay in the office."

⇶ 24 ⇷

ELIZABETH HAD BEEN OUT OF WORK A WEEK THE NIGHT EDDIE
didn't come home. He said when he left that morning that he was
doing his usual, going off to look for something around the docks
or maybe over to King Edward. When he wasn't back by midnight, she and Lenora invented all kinds of reasons for what might
have happened. An all-night job somewhere. Someone he knew
had invited him home for a late dinner. He'd fallen asleep in a
warehouse, maybe was locked inside.

When he wasn't back by the next afternoon, they went
down to the docks to look for themselves but didn't know where
to start, the three piers stretching out a thousand feet each over
the St. Johns River. Gulls dipped and swooped overhead. The air
was pungent with the smell of resin, fish, and fertilizer being
hoisted off one of the cargo ships. For a while she and Lenora
went off in different directions, talking to whoever would talk to
them up and down the piers and along the dock; but either no

one had seen him the last few days, or they didn't know who he was. They stopped by King Edward on their way back to the cafe, and, yes, they knew him, but he hadn't worked for them since the previous Thursday.

When he didn't come home that night, either, they returned to the docks the next day. They did run into a young fellow who thought he'd seen him two days before over by one of the steel warehouses back of the end pier, but even he couldn't be certain.

They asked around some of the warehouses, a manager at one of them saying, "Yeah, he worked a few hours that day and then left." They wanted to know more, but it wasn't his policy to pass out information on his workers, he said. Neither she nor Lenora trusted him, though they couldn't say why, and it left them terribly frustrated and frightened. If Eddie was in trouble, they had to help. And they had to find him to help.

Every day they went out hunting, until they ran out of money and food and had to spend time taking care of their own needs. Food seemed harder to turn up than ever, and there was no work anywhere, since hordes of people from up in the northern cities were down south for the winter.

After ten days, they reluctantly gave up, venturing out only to scrounge for food. Once Elizabeth thought she heard the window in the back room open, and she leaped up off her mattress and stood there waiting for the door to swing open. But it never did. Sometimes, when Lenora left her behind to go off to church, Elizabeth was sure the loneliness would swallow her up.

"We have to make some plans," Lenora announced one morning, rolling over on her mattress and lifting herself heavily up onto her elbows. "With Eddie gone and the food so scarce and only feeling welcome in a colored church, well, I hate to go off and leave him, but I don't see much point."

Elizabeth had had the same kind of thoughts looming in her

mind. Something had happened to Eddie; that was clear now, or he would have been back. But what? There wasn't any way of *knowing*. Burying her face in the mattress, she tried to think of what else they could do to find him, but they'd run through their ideas a hundred times. She'd been thinking, too, about why she'd left home and the fact that they weren't turning up even the remotest possibility for work. They were "striking out," as Eddie would've put it. Jacksonville was picked clean, like a dead fish on the beach.

She sat up and looked at Lenora, faced with the real possibility of her whole life changing again. "We just can't go off and leave him. What if he comes back and we're not here?"

"Elizabeth," Lenora said softly, "what else are we gonna do? Two girls alone like us are sitting ducks. We're askin' for trouble, maybe more trouble than Eddie's in. And people do starve, you know. It's more than that for me, though. I need to go back to New York. I need to try going home."

Elizabeth went out by herself, walking aimlessly around Jacksonville until she found herself down by the docks. Standing behind a rail, she watched the ships come and go for most of the afternoon, until she'd made her mind up.

When she returned toward evening, she said, "Let's go right away, then. I don't want to hang around thinking about it." She glanced around the cafe. The windows were still boarded up, but there were other small indications here and there that it had been someone's home for the winter. *Their* home. Remembering back to how she'd felt leaving her room at home back in Chicago, she realized that she hadn't spent that much time thinking about that room after all. But thinking of it now, and seeing in her mind the kitchen back home as well, with her ma and pa, Waldo and Whitney seated around the table, she felt a sudden yearning.

Lenora slipped into her sweater, saying maybe Elizabeth

could come back to New York with her. Maybe it was better for work back there now, and they'd both find something to do. Elizabeth looked into Lenora's kind brown eyes and knew how hard it would be to let her go. Then Lenora said Elizabeth ought to be sure to leave her address in Chicago for Eddie. He was sure to turn up sometime.

Elizabeth left Eddie a note. It said:

Dear Eddie:

We're sorry we couldn't wait any longer, but food got so scarce, and there's no work at all. We never found out what happened to you, but we think maybe you got picked up and they put you on a bus for Indiana. We hope that's all, and that nothing worse happened. Lenora is going to New York, and I'm off to Chicago. Maybe we'll be back, who knows? I'm sorry about taking your map, but I didn't think I could get anywhere without it. Now you have to come to Chicago to get it. I wonder if you will, or if you'll forget about me once you're somewhere else. I won't forget about you.

Yours truly,
Elizabeth and Lenora

Bye, Eddie, she thought, brushing away a tear and placing the note on the counter.

⟶⟫ 25 ⟪⟵

THE TRAIN'S ROLLING FORWARD WAS HYPNOTIC, LIKE THE CON-
stant hum of a machine. Elizabeth thought she was sewing again
and sleepily opened her eyes. "Where are we?" she asked, read-
justing the pack underneath her head.

"I suspect somewhere between Waycross and Eastman. You
been sleeping?" Lenora sat cross-legged, her back to the wall.

"Not really. I've been thinking with my eyes shut." She
swatted something buzzing around her ear.

"What you been thinking about?"

"I was remembering what this girl from work told me, that
this route is called 'the gnat line' in summer, all the way up
through the south of Georgia, because these tiny, tiny gnats
hang around your eyes. She said you get rid of them by blowing
a sharp puff of air from the corner of your mouth, and it drives
them away like a tornado, only you have to keep doing it and
doing it to keep them away." She blew out of the corner of her
mouth to demonstrate.

"Well, I'm glad it's not summer then," said Lenora.

Lenora hadn't said much since they'd left Jacksonville, mostly kept her thoughts to herself. There wasn't that much to be said anyway, having gone round and round about what could've happened to Eddie, until there was nothing left to say aloud, just private feelings. Elizabeth's worst thoughts were ones she could barely admit to herself anyway, that something really awful had happened. She wished with all her heart that he was right here with them now, shuffling cards off in a corner, coaxing her to play.

She raised herself up onto her elbows, then got all the way up and crossed the car to slide open the door, then sat down with her legs dangling over the side. Tilting her face up to the sun, inhaling the fragrance of pine from the flat woods all around them, she suddenly felt better, more hopeful. Maybe Eddie was really all right, and soon she would be home again, and everything would be fine there, too. So she wasn't coming home a hero with a bundle of money. She'd managed to send something home each week she worked and just prayed they'd got it and it had helped.

The train's whistle blared up ahead and, looking out at some houses on the crest of a low hill, she figured they could be closing in on Macon. Macon bacon. They had enough food to last them maybe through Tennessee. Then what?

"The sun feels good," said Lenora behind her. She uncrossed her legs and leaned forward, rubbing her back. "Let's leave it open."

"All right. Maybe we're past Eastman now and coming to Macon. We've got a long way to go, don't we?"

Lenora didn't answer, and Elizabeth turned to look at her.

"You know what I said about coming back with me to New York?"

"Yes?"

"Well, you couldn't really. Because where I live is all

Negroes, I mean *all* Negroes, like Decatur Street. You'd have stood out like the moon at midnight."

Elizabeth rolled the legs of each overall halfway up each calf, not sure what to say, remembering how she'd felt walking down Decatur.

"I know you wouldn't have come anyway. You need to get home to see your family. But, say you didn't have a place to go, you still couldn't come. Ah, I don't know . . . it's a mixed-up kind of world, isn't it?" Lenora stood, brushing off her skirt, and came to stand behind Elizabeth. "Look at those beautiful trees out there, thousands and thousands of them. Someday I would like just one in a yard of my own. It's a stupid thing to wish for, when you don't have anything."

"I don't think it's stupid at all," Elizabeth said softly.

Lenora rested her hand on Elizabeth's shoulder and sighed. "I just want to say it once and don't take it the wrong way, but . . . sometimes, I can't say why, I just wish you were colored."

She knew, in a way, what Lenora was trying to say, and she was filled with a sudden rush of feeling—sadness, longing, and love. Her whole last year had been one separation after another. She looked up at Lenora. "You wish we didn't have to go off in opposite directions."

"Yeah, it's going to be hard to leave you, but the Lord giveth, and the Lord taketh away."

Elizabeth swallowed, reaching up to clasp Lenora's warm, familiar hand, as the train click-clacked along, steaming its way through southern Georgia, up past Atlanta, on into the Smokies in Tennessee, eventually through Knoxville and then Kentucky. Just before they reached Cincinnati, Lenora jumped off to catch a train going east to New York. Leaning out away from the freight car as far as she could without falling, Elizabeth watched her become a small speck along the side of the tracks, until they

182

passed through a long, dark tunnel. When they emerged from the other end, she'd disappeared from view.

Elizabeth sat in a circle of soft light pouring through where a slat in the wall of the boxcar had rotted away, her arms wrapped around her chest to keep in her body heat. Like the boxcar's buckling underneath her, her longings drew her first forward to Chicago, then back to the cafe in Jacksonville, and homeward to Chicago again.

As the afternoon light faded from the color of wheat to a light rose, she began to walk to stay warm. Back and forth down the center of the car and all around the sides in a rectangle. Every time the train stopped or slowed she held her breath, hoping the door wouldn't slide open to admit a stranger. When she warmed up from walking, she lay down to try to sleep, but the wind sweeping through the holes in the slats made it almost impossible. Once she awoke to find powdery white patches where the holes were big enough to let snow in.

She was too cold and hungry to make it through the night and jumped off when she saw a scattering of lights piercing the darkness outside. The snow was about a foot deep, and she began to trudge through it along a road, passing a few small houses, a filling station, and a few truck stops. By following in the tire tracks of passing trucks and cars on the hardened snow, she was able to make better time. But better time to *where* she wasn't sure, hoping maybe to stumble on another church with an open door.

Elizabeth hunched against the frigid wind, which every now and then would snap at her face as though it had teeth, driving the snow down under her collar and up the legs of her overalls. The light jacket that had served her just fine in Florida seemed useless, even with her sweater underneath. After a mile or so she came to a friendly looking little diner aglow with a soft buttery-yellow light, and she was too weary to pass it by.

A middle-aged woman stood behind the counter, reading a magazine. "Holler when you know what you want," she mumbled, glancing at Elizabeth to give her a quick once-over.

Elizabeth carefully removed both her shoes and her socks, remembering Eddie's stories of toes and fingers lost to winter cold. Eddie. She rubbed her hands and feet vigorously, beginning to feel sensation return, then leaned her head against the back of the booth and closed her eyes. Eddie and Lenora both gone.

"Where you coming from?"

She hadn't heard the woman come up to the table.

"Jacksonville," she replied, trying to rouse herself to attention.

"Jacksonville?" The woman's red lips parted in surprise. She withdrew a pad of checks from her apron pocket. "That's a long ways from Indianapolis. Where're you headed?"

Elizabeth took a deep breath and exhaled. "Chicago."

The woman looked at her intently, as though making up her mind. "Gimme your socks, your shoes, and your jacket," she finally said. "I'll warm them up by the radiator."

Elizabeth stayed two nights, sleeping under a wool blanket on a cot in the back room, doing the dishes in the daytime in return for food.

On the morning she was to leave, Josephine and her husband borrowed a neighbor's car to drive her to the train, although she'd told them she didn't mind walking. But they wouldn't take no. When they stopped the car it was in front of a large, wooden building downtown. She looked all around for the tracks, the cinders, an old red-brown boxcar with C&O up the sides.

Josephine dug a five-dollar bill from her purse, handing it to Elizabeth across the back seat.

"No, thanks," said Elizabeth. "Really."

"You can't ride for nothing," said her husband. "Go'wan now, or she'll be late for work."

Josephine smiled. "You'll hit Chicago tonight. Have a good ride."

Elizabeth slid out from the back seat, thanking them profusely, astounded at their kindness. In a half hour she had her ticket, leaning back into a regular seat on a Pullman. She was "ridin' passenger" the rest of the way home. No railroad detectives could bother her now. Blue-uniformed conductors hung around the steps, waiting for late arrivals. Colored porters pushed baggage carts behind decent-looking people all on their way to somewhere.

Though she figured she didn't look decent at all, she was on her way to somewhere, too.

➤➤➤ 26 ◄◄◄

SHE REMOVED EDDIE'S MAP FROM HER PACK AS THE TRAIN ROLLED
gently out of the station. There was Indianapolis, like a bull's-eye
in the middle of the state. Then she scanned the rest of Indiana,
playing their old game. Pilot Knob, Cementville, Lamb, Patriot,
Gnaw Bone, Roachdale, Raccoon, Young America, Domestic,
Brushy Prairie. . . . Gnaw Bone. She wanted to say them out loud
and she wanted Eddie and Lenora to hear them and laugh. She
looked for Kokomo, Eddie's town, and there it was, a neat yellow
square a few inches above Indianapolis. Maybe he was there now,
and if she got off, she could find him. But she didn't think she
could wander around one more new town cold and hungry, and
especially alone. Maybe she would find his name in a phone book
after she returned to Chicago and write to him then.

For long stretches of time the landscape out her window was
broken only by farmhouses and barns, the silos poking up out of
the flat white shimmering fields like red swollen fingers. The snow

186

was so white and so bright it hurt to keep on looking. She saw a dead dog on the cinder bed, the Lafayette town square wrapped in gray slush, a family living in a rusted-out shell of an automobile, covered bridges spanning frozen rivers and streams. Soon the gray, towering steel mills of Gary loomed ahead, like a southern fortress to the city of Chicago. Then came Calumet City, South Holland, Blue Island, and Chicago itself. Department stores, churches and parks, gray office buildings against a slate blue sky. The names floated by outside the window: Smithy's Smoked Ribs and the Holy Redeemer Church, the American Legion and the Wildcat Lounge.

She stepped off the train in Union Station around five-thirty.

WELCOME TO THE CITY OF CHICAGO
HOME OF THE 1933 WORLD'S FAIR
"A CENTURY OF PROGRESS"

After racing up the steps of the station, she crossed over to La Salle Street, past the newsmen hawking papers, and the greasy hamburger joints and roasted hot dog stands, hardly even aware of her hunger. She'd forgotten how noisy a big city could be and clasped her hands over her ears as the elevated trains roared and clanged on the tracks above.

The wind off the lakefront sent her hurrying past restaurants and theaters, their marquees ablaze for the evening, and down darkening streets to the terminal on Van Buren.

"Destination?" the woman behind the window crisply repeated. It was 15 cents to ride the Illinois Central down to the 111th Street station. Elizabeth counted the money in her pocket and then changed her mind, leaving the station and heading through thinning crowds away from the lakefront toward the Chicago River. After crossing a bridge, she saw a water tank up ahead and rusty iron rails running along through the dirty snow. Hovering beside the water tank to block the wind, she blew on her hands and stomped her feet to keep warm. When a train heading south came rolling by, she jogged alongside for a hundred feet or so, then leaped for the handholds running up the side of a passing freight car.

The old neighborhood glowed fuzzily under the streetlamps as she hurried along with her head down, the cold air freezing her breath. The old Rothman house still looked vacant, a sled rested against a porch rail at the Swensens', and the same streetlamp bulb was out toward the end of the block. There were lights on behind the drapery at Vera's old place, but she knew it wouldn't be the Vanhorns inside having dinner.

The snow in front of her own house hadn't been shoveled, squeaking and crunching beneath her feet as she took the steps two at a time. The house was dark and there were no curtains.

She wasn't sure how long she stood there, the snow melting beneath her feet, seeping in to dampen her socks, numb her toes. Maybe until she heard Lenora whisper, "The Lord giveth and the Lord taketh away."

She leaned over the rail and once again pressed her face to the glass, her breath steaming a little portholelike clearing in the frost. It was the same every time. The house was empty. She looked and looked, as though looking would fill it all up again, until she almost started to see the old green sofa against the wall, the floor lamp beside it, and the glass-topped coffee table strewn with newspapers. Then she stopped looking and turned and went back down the steps.

She tromped around to the back of the house through the snow, hoping to see Waldo's bicycle or a snow shovel perched up against the side, but it was just the side of an empty house and nothing more. Then she crossed the street and knocked on the Swensen door, but there was no answer. She cut across the front yard to the Rosetti house. The older sister, Katherine, opened the door. Her hands flew to her face in surprise, as though Elizabeth had come back from the dead.

"Oh, my, it's Elizabeth!" she shrieked. "Poor child, come in!"

Elizabeth shook her head. "Do you know where they are?" she quavered. "There's nobody inside, and no furniture. . . ." She could smell the inside of the house, and it smelled like a home. Like heat and something cooking.

"Oh . . . oh, dear," Katherine stammered, pulling at a wisp of white hair. "They got a Public Defender to help them, but . . . I saw your ma at the market. Oh, everybody's leaving . . . if we didn't own this already. . . ." It seemed she was about to cry.

"Could you tell me where they went?"

"Corner of Wentworth and 110th, upstairs. You'll come back to visit, won't you?"

She ran to the corner of 110th and Wentworth with the moon behind her, casting a hunched-up shadow across her path. 110th and Wentworth consisted of one empty lot and three corner buildings—two houses and one brownstone two-flat. She crossed the street slowly. There was a light on toward the front of the upstairs apartment. She climbed the cement steps one at a time, then rang the bell.

Elizabeth heard the stairs creak and saw through the curtain over the window in the door a partially visible figure descending the stairs. The curtain parted to reveal half of her mother's face and the door flew open.

⇶ 27 ⇷

ELIZABETH SET THE BAG OF POTATOES ON THE TABLE. MAYBE HER mother meant to use them for stew, or soup, she thought, and went to the icebox to see what was in it. She couldn't seem to *not* inspect the icebox and cupboards each day, even if she knew the same things were probably in them as the day before.

"What's in the bag?" Waldo stepped out of the small room he shared with Whitney and into the kitchen.

"Potatoes." She was still staring at the shelves inside the icebox.

"Waldo keeps forgetting to empty the pan under the icebox," said Carl. "That's why the tile around it is always wet." He poured an inch of amber liquid into a glass and put the bottle back up in the cupboard.

"We'll both try to remember, won't we?" She winked at her brother and he smiled sheepishly back.

"And the plumbing in this place must've been done by an

Irishman. Ha! I say that to your ma a lot and she gets mad." He downed the whiskey and slapped the glass on the counter. "You've seen what happens with that thing's supposed to be a toilet, haven't you? We could go fishing in our own bathroom any night of the week."

Her father's hair fell across his forehead like a young boy's, but she thought his face had aged since summer. She glanced back down at the potatoes on the table, wondering if she should peel them. Maybe her ma meant to bake them. Potatoes and what? She checked the cupboard again.

"You've got a fishing pole, don't you, Pa?" Waldo leaned against the doorjamb, smiling. He'd grown taller, she was sure. There were at least a couple of inches between the hem of his pants and the tops of his shoes.

"Boots, too, and we'll need them." Carl rubbed the stubble on his chin, spit in the sink, and ran the faucet. "I'm sorry you had to come back to a place like this, Elizabeth." He stared into the bottom of his glass and sighed. "We did our best and look what still happened."

"It's all right, Pa. I'm just glad to be back." She took the potatoes to the sink, thinking once more about the old house and how she missed it. But she never let on, and compared to some of the places she'd lived in . . . Her ma told her they'd received $300 from the bank folks when they'd had to move out. That was all they got back even though they'd had half the mortgage paid off.

"I'm glad you're back, too. You're a lot more important than a house."

She turned and kissed her father on his scratchy cheek, then followed Waldo around the corner into his room, where he'd built a tent with blankets up over his bed. Her ma said he seldom came out of his room since they'd moved, that he hadn't been interested in meeting new friends or playing out in the snow. Since she was back home, he'd been following her around the house like a puppy.

"Show me that farm, where you picked tobacco." He looked up at Eddie's map, which she'd hung on his wall.

"It's right here," she pointed.

"The farmer's wife made apple pie once," Waldo added. "And you lived in the barracks."

"That's right."

"Here's where you first saw the ocean." He pointed to a spot on the Florida coast. "Florida. Now where'd you sleep in that shed?"

"Up here, in Atlanta." She did not tell him, or anyone else, about the rest of her stay in Atlanta. She wondered if she'd even tell Vera.

"Yeah, that was good pie," she said. "I was real hungry, because right before then is where we had that chicken claw stew, and that's all there was for days, and I didn't much like it." She didn't want him to get any ideas of his own, to think she'd been on vacation and he could go next.

"*Yuk.*"

"That's what *I* said."

"This isn't a tent anymore. See how I've squared it off at the corners? It's a boxcar. Want to get in?"

She climbed underneath the blankets, careful not to dislodge the broom and yardstick at either end holding them up. "This is nice," she said. "Your bed sure makes it soft, though. Maybe you ought to put it on the floor and sleep down there to make it more real."

He paused, looking at the bare wood and thinking. "I guess I could try it."

"I'm taking you to the Fair," she announced. "There's a special deal for kids this Saturday. How does that sound?"

At that his face fell, and she lifted his chin with her hand. "What's wrong? I know you haven't been to it yet."

He yanked his face away, scowling. "We *can't* go to the Fair. You been gone, so you don't know, but we don't have the money for nothin' no more!"

"I've saved the money for just this, Waldo. Honest I have!"

"Is that why you *left*, to earn money to go to the Fair?" His eyes widened and he burst into tears.

She pulled him close and wrapped her arms around his shoulders. "No, I went away to work, like I told you, to help ma and dad out. I just saved something for us, that's all." She held him an arm's length away and smiled, brushing a few tears off his cheeks.

One of the hardest things about being back home was that her ma and pa didn't *want* to know more about what she'd been through. She'd spent the first few days thinking about how much she'd tell them, how she'd answer their questions, but after a while she realized they weren't going to ask her anything. She tried to pique their interest, tempt them with bits of information.

"These overalls I'm wearing were given to me by a farmer's wife in Virginia."

"Is that so? Well, that was nice of her," said Esther one night at dinner. "Please pass the bread, Carl."

"You know farmers can't sell anything nowadays," she tried again. "I saw that everywhere I went. For two dollars you could buy a *live* pig, a live sheep for a dollar."

"Imagine," said Esther.

"Oh, come on," said Waldo.

"I'm not kidding."

"What would you do with it then?" he continued.

"Eat it." She looked around the table, waiting.

"You may eat now, Waldo," said Carl.

She could at least count on Waldo for questions. Her ma and pa didn't want to know about live pigs or dead ones. They wanted to talk about her going back to school and to forget that she'd ever been gone, maybe forget what could have happened. Or perhaps enough had happened to them already and they didn't want to face anything more.

"You know," Esther said thoughtfully, turning to Elizabeth. "There's that small yard behind our building. We could . . . we could plant a garden together this summer. Like we've always done before?"

"Yeah, that's a good idea." She tried to sound enthusiastic for her mother's sake. But it would never be like before.

Once when Esther was out at a church club meeting, her father peered at her over his newspaper and asked her a question about her job. She leaned toward him eagerly in the small living room and told him all about it.

"I can sew now, Pa. Maybe now I could get a sewing job around here and help out."

"You're going back to school, Elizabeth. I know you mean well, but that's all there is to it."

"We still need the money, maybe now more than ever."

"Yer a stubborn Swede like me. Go to school, so you don't become a janitor." The paper went up, shielding his face.

"There's nothing wrong with being a janitor. What's wrong is food rotting in the fields while people starve everywhere, and . . ."

"Yer a tough ol' Swede; that's good." Then he put the paper down and reached to turn on the radio, sitting on a small table beside the sofa. "It took me two weeks to put this thing back together again. Listen," he whispered. "It's 'Little Orphan Annie.' That was you for a while, wasn't it? Don't ever go away like that again, Elizabeth. Come listen."

One of her mother's entries in the Betty Crocker cake competition had won an honorable mention. She received a free five-pound bag of the new Gold Medal flour as a prize and baked a cake one night, inviting the Vanhorns over to surprise Elizabeth.

Nobody looked exactly as she remembered them. Vera's bust line was bigger and her hairstyle longer and fuller. Elizabeth was glad to see her, hoping to find in Vera a willing listener, but as soon as they were alone together out for a walk, she felt awkward, unsure of herself. How could she possibly begin, and where?

"How's school?" she began, as they stepped along slowly, planting their feet where the sidewalk showed through in the hardened gray snow.

"Pretty good," Vera replied, pulling her scarf up to cover her chin. "I'm going to try out for a small part in a play this spring, see if it'll help me get over being shy. The kids at school kept asking about you, if I thought you had to go away to have a baby." She looked at Elizabeth's face and laughed. Elizabeth shuddered, thinking about going back to face them.

"I didn't know what to tell them," Vera went on, her voice hardening a bit. "I thought maybe I should let them think you were pregnant. I mean, here you were mad at me that day we had to move because I hadn't told you ahead of time. And then you go off one day and you don't come back and I never hear a *word* from you." Her curls swung from side to side above her collar as she walked. "I was sure you were *dead.* Then I heard from my ma you ran away to Florida, to get this job."

"I didn't run away," Elizabeth replied, biting her lip. "I'm sorry, though . . . I didn't tell anyone."

Vera came to a dead stop, stuffing her fists into her coat pockets. "Look, Elizabeth, I have to tell you something. I wasn't going to say anything, but I have to." She stared down at the sidewalk and then took a deep breath. "This is hard, but, well . . . last summer I wished you'd lose your house, too, right after we did. It was terrible going through that, and I wanted you to know what it was like. But I don't think I really wanted it to happen to you, too. And now it has. I'm sorry. I just had to get it off my conscience."

Elizabeth looked off into the distance, through a tunnel of bare branches, where the rows of houses merged into a single thin line at the horizon. "I just can't believe we're not going back. That it's gone for good."

"I'm sorry," Vera said again and put her hand on Elizabeth's shoulder.

"I don't blame you for thinking that last summer, Vera. I wasn't at all nice to you. Maybe it was because I didn't want to know anyone who was poor. I was just afraid, and I'm sorry." She stopped and turned and threw her arms around Vera's neck.

"That'd be pretty hard nowadays, wouldn't it?" said Vera, as they separated and continued down the sidewalk. "To not know someone who's poor. Look, I just want to know everything that happened to you, if you'll tell me. . . ."

"I do want to tell you, starting with how I met Eddie right here in the neighborhood. . . ."

"*Eddie?* My ma didn't mention an 'Eddie'!"

Elizabeth laughed, kicking a chunk of ice into a pile of slush, and took a deep breath. A snowball whizzed past her head. She turned, as Waldo came running up behind them. "I guess we'll have to finish this later. . . ."

On the following Saturday, she and Waldo rode an open double-decker bus to the Adler Planetarium, the Fair stretching from there for three miles up along the lakefront. Once inside, she couldn't decide what to take him to first: the South African diamond mine, the Chinese temple, Treasure Island, boat rides, the Sears Pavilion with electric-eye drinking fountains, television, the first streamlined, aluminum railroad car. . . . Whatever it cost, the whole day was worth one glimpse at the rapture in Waldo's face as the Sky Ride Rocket cars transported them high above the Fair, higher than any building in Chicago.

They stayed just past dusk to observe the Arcturus lighting ceremony at the Court of the Hall of Science Pavilion.

"Somebody somewhere pushes a button and the light from the star Arcturus, way, way out there, is used to light all the lights of the Fair every night," she explained. She clasped his hand as they waited among the crowds. "It took forty years for the light from this star to get here."

"Naah. Not *forty*," he said, looking up into the darkening sky.

"Yes, forty. Please stop talking out of the side of your mouth. You look like a gangster. The light we'll see was out there in space and now it's about to arrive here."

At just that moment the lights burst on all around them. "First there was darkness, and then there was light," she whispered. She squeezed Waldo's hand, trying to comprehend the vastness of space, the speed of light, who she might be in forty years. . . .

⇶ Epilogue ⇷

WHEN I LOOK BACK TO THE YEAR OF 1933 I WONDER HOW I COULD have done such a thing, left the family I loved so much to go off with a strange boy I had no reason to trust, to become a "sister of the road." I guess I've come to believe we're capable of most anything if desperate enough.

My father went back to work full time in a machine shop in 1936. Things were a lot better for us, but we couldn't get far enough ahead to buy another house. I got a steady after-school job myself in the spring of '35, running paper through a glue machine in a bookbindery at 14th and Michigan Avenue. When I graduated in 1936 I went to work in an insurance office downtown in the Loop, not far from the office on La Salle where I'd applied for that dancing job at the Fair. Now I'm one of those people, head buried in a newspaper, riding the train every day. Except I look up each time we pass through the slums.

On September 6, 1934, almost a year to the day since I'd met him, I received a letter from Eddie (I have all his letters before me right now) and was so upset to find out that he'd spent six months in a Florida work camp. On the day that he'd disappeared, he wrote that he was able to find a few hours of work in a warehouse, just like Lenora and I had assumed. But before he left for the day, he'd gotten in a fight over money with the boss, who called the cops and had him hauled away as a "troublemaker." When he got out, Lenora and I were gone, of course, and he said prison "had done something to his head." He was too ashamed to try to look me up, to see me right then face-to-face.

In '35 he hired on with the government's new Civilian Conservation Corps and went to work out west in the forests of Washington State, sending most of the money home. After that he got a good job as a welder, met a girl, and got engaged. I have often wondered about her, what she's like. But now, with war rumors coming on, he's enlisted. I'll just hope he does all right for himself, wherever he is.

I never heard from Lenora, even though I sent postcards to all the Hendrys I could find listed in Harlem. Whenever I think of her, I see her face across the table at the Coming Home Cafe, and I remember what she said about the colored Depression being worse than ours, and I hope it didn't swallow her up.

It's 1939. Another World's Fair is taking place in New York. The real world itself seems to be going to war again; there's a lunatic named Hitler terrorizing Europe.

With so much happening in the world, I think I'd like to get more schooling, get a job as a reporter with a big newspaper. I remember Joan Crawford in a movie years ago, solving some important case as a cub reporter. Oh, I know it wouldn't be like that. I know the difference between movies and real life, between movie heroes and real heroes and heroines. It's just human nature, though, to hope for a better life, no matter the odds against it.